THE SEDUCTRESS

Song of the Sirens 1

Morgan Ashbury

EROTIC ROMANCE

Siren Publishing, Inc.
www.SirenPublishing.com

A SIREN PUBLISHING BOOK
IMPRINT: Erotic Romance

THE SEDUCTRESS
Song of the Sirens 1
Copyright © 2008 by Morgan Ashbury

ISBN-10: 1-60601-409-9
ISBN-13: 978-1-60601-409-7

First Publication: December 2008

Cover design by Jinger Heaston
All cover art and logo copyright © 2008 by Siren Publishing, Inc.

Printed in the U.S.A.

PUBLISHER
Siren Publishing, Inc.
www.SirenPublishing.com

DEDICATION

To Selena, the siren who captured my Christopher's heart.

THE SEDUCTRESS

Song of the Sirens 1

Morgan Ashbury
Copyright © 2008

Prologue

In life we were The Sirens, exiled by the gods of Olympus to a rocky island, there to lure men to their end. Now in death we finally have the chance to be heard. Yes, it is true we did not at first raise the alarm when Persephone was taken by Hades. She asked us to say nothing, for love had drawn her to the lord of the underworld. When she did not return, we searched for her, but to no avail. We could not follow where she had been taken. And Demeter, in her anger, condemned us.

Here, as there, we stand united. We are sisters, we three, of the heart if not of the blood. And we face three sisters, for surely the Moerae are that, though I doubt there is a single heart among them.

We have won this audience to plead our case, but I already know the outcome. How this can be so, I do not understand. In life I had no gift of sight, though it had been said my grandmother could hear the call of the oracle. Beside me, Ligeia trembles, even as Thelxiope holds as still as marble. And I, Peisinoe, mourn for those mortal women as yet unborn, those three we will become again and again throughout the millennia, waiting for the curse we are about to receive to be broken. I acknowledge the irony in my heart, for once more gods decide and the innocent are powerless against them. And so we will be bound, century upon century, until we succeed in winning the hearts of men who believe we have betrayed them.

   Three women. Three destinies. One fate.

Chapter 1

"I don't get it."

The words held such a note of puzzlement, Pamela Singer smiled even as she turned to look at the man who'd spoken them.

The expression of confusion on his face matched perfectly the tone of his voice. He stood taller than her five-foot-seven frame, with black hair long enough to brush his collar. His eyes, an electric blue, drew her gaze almost hypnotically. The gods must have given him that chiselled visage, that classic male beauty. She tried very hard not to notice *how* good-looking he was. Neither did she acknowledge to herself—overmuch—that something about him put a hum in her bloodstream. Because looking at him was far more pleasing than it should be, she turned her attention instead to the painting he was studying.

The piece, entitled "Dawn Hybrid," was one the Langdon Gallery in Philadelphia had only recently acquired. Considered a fine example of the Minimalist style and painted in the early nineteen seventies, the painting had been purchased from a private collector. Judging by the way the gallery had showcased the piece, they considered it the cornerstone of their Twentieth Century American collection.

The man turned to her, and Pamela tried in vain to lasso her hormones. Gazing at him in profile had been thrill enough. Seeing him eye-to-eye was almost too much.

"I just don't get it," he said again. "This isn't art. It's…lines on a canvas. This could have been turned out by any third-grader in any school in the country."

Normally, Pamela's love of art would cause her hackles to rise at the sound of such heresy. But for some reason, that sentiment from this man, looking truly confused and adorable as he expressed it didn't incite her ire at all. Laughing softly, she looked at the painting, trying to see it through his eyes.

"Not many people are fans of the Minimalist style."

"Minimalist, is it? Usually, I agree with the concept that less is more. But in this case…"

He smiled at her, and when her heart gave a little lurch, Pamela knew she was in deep trouble. Just when she thought she couldn't sink any farther, a look of chagrin crossed his face.

"Um…I didn't just insult you or anything, did I?"

Before she could answer, he continued on. "Hell, of course I did. Sorry. My mother spent a lot of time taking me through art galleries, and so I understand more than most that art is in the eye of the beholder. Dylan Pierce." He held out his hand.

Looking from his now-hopeful expression to his outstretched hand, Pamela knew that she was completely captivated. *You would think that after what happened with Dmitri, I'd know better.* With a sense of inevitability, she accepted the handshake.

"You really didn't offend me, though I should have been. Pamela Singer."

"I think you're just being generous."

He flashed another smile and then turned his attention back to the art. "I don't hate art, really. I just don't understand it. My idea of what defines art is probably old-fashioned. You know, fruit in a bowl, portraits, that sort of thing."

"What about Impressionism?"

"Is that where it *almost* looks like real things but the edges are fuzzed?"

Pamela had never heard the style described in quite that way before. She couldn't hold back her laugh. "Yes, that would be it."

He tilted his head to one side and shot her a look she thought should belong to a little boy trying to worm some treat.

"You have a nice laugh." As if realizing that was perhaps too personal an observation, he broke eye contact, looked back at the painting for a moment, then turned back to her. "Mother tried her best to educate me, but for reasons unknown, my brain refused to absorb details or acquire appreciation. All I really know about art is that I like what I like. And this unfortunately is not it."

"That's fair enough. But I have to ask you, that being the case, what are you doing here?"

"We made a large donation to the Langdon to finance this exhibit. As an executive vice president, it was my duty to come and see it."

Pamela tilted her head, something she knew she did when trying to recall details. "You're with the Carstairs Hotel Group?"

"I am. Rather unavoidable since my paternal grandmother is Eugenia Carstairs."

This meant, Pamela reflected, that he came from money, and lots of it. "I'd heard your grandmother retired recently to some place exotic…the Mediterranean, was it?"

"Gran doesn't know the meaning of the word retirement."

There was a wealth of affection in his voice, and Pamela felt her heart melt a little more. This was dangerous. All she had to do was look back a few short months to know just how dangerous letting down her guard could be. She'd opened her heart to Dmitri Andropolis, fallen completely under his spell. That transformation hadn't happened in just a few minutes in an art gallery, either, but had developed over several weeks.

She was still smarting from his fit of temper, although the bruises had long since faded. No man, not even any of her former foster fathers, had ever hit her before.

Pamela was no one's victim. She'd turned her back and walked away from Dmitri, despite the fact she'd been in love with him. He'd tried to apologize, of course, but after a few weeks had finally understood there would be no second chance from her.

She brought her attention back to the present. Dylan seemed different than any man she'd ever met. The information he'd given as to his identity had been done without airs, as a normal part of the conversation. Any man whose voice softened at the mention of his mother and grandmother was, she decided, a man worth getting to know a bit better. Who knew, he might make a good friend.

She had her sisters, of course, but few other friends at the moment. The only question was could she keep him in that position?

"I think that's wonderful," she said now in response to his comment about his grandmother. "Too many people think the elderly should just...go sit in a rocking chair somewhere."

Dylan chuckled. "I'm trying to picture Gran in a rocker. Nope, the picture just won't form. She still walks five miles every day. I hope I'm that agile when I'm in my eighties."

"Haven't you heard? Sixty is the new forty. At least that was one of the headlines flashing on my ISP's home page this morning."

"That seems about right. Listen, I really do feel bad about my insensitive comments with regard to this..." He seemed at a loss for words as he looked at the painting again. Pamela laughed, and it felt good.

"Let's just call it a painting. And there's no need to apologize, really."

"Well, rats. I was hoping to tempt you into joining me for a cup of coffee in the restaurant here. For which I would pay, of course, as a token of my...um...remorse."

"I bet you get your way a lot when you use that puppy-dog look."

Dylan's laugh, soft, low, and natural did interesting things to her heart rate.

"Busted. Ms. Singer, may I please buy you a cup of coffee?"

Well, hell. Even without the cute, little boy-slash-sad puppy face, he got to her. Pamela did want to spend just a little bit more time in this intriguing man's company. He made her laugh, and she could always use more laughter in her life.

He wasn't the type of man she usually spent her time with. For one thing, he didn't wear that sheen of polish and sophistication that covered some of the nouveau riche, and the old money types, too. His nose wasn't in the air, and not a speck of arrogance was in sight. Dressed in Levis and a collared shirt, he wore the casual attire with the ease of familiarity and comfort.

She'd bet he didn't have a sterling silver money clip to his name.

He was close to her own age, whereas most of the men who'd engaged her interest and intellect over the last few years had been decades older.

She imagined a shrink would have a field day with that admission.

In short, Dylan seemed to be, despite his wealth, a really nice guy. What would it hurt to share a cup of coffee with a really nice guy?

"Thank you, Mr. Pierce. A cup of coffee sounds great."

* * * *

Dylan could certainly see why his brother had fallen for her. Hair the color of rich chocolate framed what he could only call a sweetheart face. Her aqua eyes had startled him, and then when they focused on him, shock had turned to captivation.

Keeping his smile in place, he sent an urgent mental memo to his libido. Don't think of Pamela Singer as a woman. Think of her as a…a *what*? *An enemy*?

The label had been an accurate one right up until she'd turned those amazing orbs on him and smiled. Hers was a smile that animated her entire face, bringing her dimples to life and sending star-like reflections to her eyes. Dylan tried to dismiss the affect she had on him as he walked with her to the elevator.

The lunch rush appeared over in the cozy restaurant on the second floor of the museum. The hostess showed them to a table next to the windows, overlooking the sculpture garden. Dylan offered lunch, but Pamela declined. When the waitress appeared, they both ordered only coffee. She returned in moments with the beverage.

"Have you been in Philadelphia long?" Pamela asked.

He had no business taking note of her full, kissable lips let alone reacting to them. The idea formed that maybe he had taken on more than he could handle with her. Focusing on her question, he decided he'd be better off to answer her truthfully, whenever he could.

"As a matter of fact, no. I missed the States, so about a week ago I flew over from London. I have friends in Philly, whom I haven't seen for a couple of years. I have to say, your city hasn't changed as much as I thought it might have." All true, as far as it went. But the more *complete* truth was that he only decided to come to Philadelphia after he'd discovered that Pamela was bound for here, from Paris.

"I'm afraid it's not my city. I *did* grow up here, but I've been living in Europe for the last few years. I'm on vacation." She gave him a little half smile that did things to his belly. Putting his chin on his hand, he tried to give the appearance of hanging on her every word and realized that there was no work at all involved in the exercise.

"But I'm rather at a crossroads," she continued on. "Not sure what I'm going to do next. I finished up my last contract. I've got offers, but I just don't know what comes next."

"Contract? For what?"

"I'm a painting conservator."

Dylan knew what that was, of course. He'd been nothing less than honest when he told Pamela that his mother had taken him around galleries all his life. The gallery his mother ran in Athens had hired a firm a couple of summers ago to restore one of their Renaissance pieces.

"That's very exacting work. Are you with one of the larger conservatories, then?"

"No, I freelance—which suits me. I can pick and choose. There's always a museum looking for someone to help them restore their treasures. And I like working alone. I like it best when it's just me and the work."

"I can see that you do." Her entire face had lit up as soon as she began to talk about her profession. "Are you a frustrated artist? Never mind. That sounded rather scurrilous."

Her laughter washed over him, a modern day Siren's song that was drawing him in. Dylan realized he was in serious trouble.

"That was a reasonable question, really. And the answer is no. Oh, I picked up charcoal and pastels a time or two in college, but I really don't have any great calling—or any great talent. No, the part that captivates me is the mystery of it all. When you begin to work with a painting, you first need to be a detective. Most of the art I've had under my hands has been worked on in the past. You need to see what has been done and look for the original artist's touch. The philosophy of art conservation has changed over the years. Now, whatever I do has to be reversible."

There it was again, a shiver of passion lacing her words. If Dylan didn't know better, he'd swear that Pamela Singer was a forthright young woman dedicated to her career. Of course, he did know better, and it was time for him to remind himself why he was there in the first place. Sharing a cup of coffee was a step in the right direction, but it was only a step. If he had any hope of carrying out his plan, he'd have to go a lot farther down this trail than a cup of coffee.

"So you're on vacation. Is your dance card full? Or does a lonely hotel exec stand a chance?"

Merriment twinkled in her eyes as she copied his pose of moments before. Palm supporting her chin, she scrutinized him for a time before asking, "Stand a chance at what?"

He sat forward and pitched his voice low. "I was thinking dinner, maybe dancing, maybe a walk along the river."

"Those sound like fun activities. You should have a good time."

"They are and I will. But I'd have an even better time if you came with me."

"Indeed?"

She was nearly laughing now, and Dylan found her humor infectious. He gave in to the urge and chuckled.

"Ms. Singer, would you have dinner with me tonight?"

The humor left her face, and he wondered what serious turn her thoughts had taken. His heart tripped and his breath caught when he thought she was going to say no.

"I can't tonight. But I'm free tomorrow night."

"Wonderful."

Dylan told himself the relief he was feeling was entirely due to his plans falling into place and had nothing whatsoever to do with the prospect of spending tomorrow evening in the company of a beautiful and appealing woman.

He would be a fool if his motivation was the latter and not the former. Beautiful and appealing Pamela Singer may very well be, but she was also something else.

She was the woman who had broken his brother's heart and ruined his reputation.

Chapter 2

It was a good thing she had said no for tonight.

Captivating aqua eyes and a certain seductive smile kept playing with his libido and short-circuiting his thoughts. Pouring himself a drink, Dylan Pierce thought it was way past time to step back and put everything into perspective.

Wandering over to the floor-to-ceiling windows in his penthouse suite at the Philadelphia Riverfront Carstairs Hotel, he watched as twilight began to fall along the Delaware River and Penn's Landing, and he remembered.

Practically from the day he'd been born, his half brother had been his hero. Older than him by ten years, Dmitri had been his defender against bullies, and a faithful playmate, allowing him to tag along endlessly. When Dylan had been fifteen, he'd copped one of his father's bottles of scotch, determined to prove himself a man. It had been Dmitri who'd held his head as he'd thrown-up the booze, and Dmitri who'd then replaced the bottle so his father wouldn't know. A year later, when he'd been in lust for the first time, it had been Dmitri he'd gone to for advice and condoms, and Dmitri who'd consoled him when the relationship had ended badly.

For all of his growing-up years, he'd known his big brother was in his corner. Considering they'd been only half siblings, that was an amazing thing in Dylan's estimation.

There wasn't anything Dylan wouldn't do for his brother.

True, Dmitri had always been moody and temperamental, but Dylan had never counted it against him. He'd been blessed to have been born into and raised in a two-parent family, a family that was loving and rock-steady. Dmitri's father had left him and their mother when his half brother had been just five years old. Even now, fully grown, Dylan couldn't say how he might have turned out if his early years had been like his brother's.

When Dmitri had been fired last month from his position with the family company for embezzling funds, Dylan had been shocked and deeply concerned. While it was true over the years his brother had shown a dislike for authority figures—he'd been thrown out of a few private schools and had nearly been arrested once—Dylan never would have thought he could ever be guilty of stealing from his own family.

It had taken him days to pry the story out of his brother. Dmitri had fallen deeply in love with a woman, one with a reputation for seducing older men and helping herself to their fortunes. Of course, Dmitri hadn't believed the outrageous stories about her at first. Then, he told Dylan, when he began to get a glimmer that those rumors might indeed be truth, he'd believed that this time, things would be different. *He* would be different. But in the end, this woman—Pamela Singer—had betrayed him, taking money from him that had been in his trust only temporarily.

Dylan had never known Dmitri to become so involved with a woman. He must have truly been in love with Pamela.

Which made her betrayal of him all the more cruel and worthy of revenge.

Dylan had urged his brother to report the matter to the police, but he'd refused. He had, he said, no proof, only his word. That commodity didn't seem to be held very highly at the moment.

But that didn't mean Dylan couldn't act. He wasn't sure how he was going to do it, but before he was through, he was determined to not only recover that half-million dollars and redeem his brother's honor, but also reveal Pamela Singer for the viper she was.

That thought didn't fit as well this evening as it had only scant days ago. Before he could think anymore about that, the phone rang.

"Pierce."

"Hunter here. What in the name of all that's holy are you doing in Philadelphia?"

Dylan's face split into a huge smile. Hunter Symington had been with the Moerae Corporation since just after his father had created it from the family business his maternal grandfather had given him. One of both his parents' closest friends, he'd been an honorary uncle to Dylan all his life. What made Hunter even more special in Dylan's eyes was that the fact that he was the only other person in the company who loved Dmitri. Hunter was the only person with whom he'd shared the details he'd pried out of his brother.

"The French have a saying," he told the older man now. "Cherchez la femme."

"Look for the woman. Ah, you're going after Dmitri's paramour. In Philadelphia? I thought she was in Paris. Does your brother know you're doing this?"

"I found out by chance that she was coming here and got here ahead of her. And no, I haven't told Dmitri. He'd only tell me to leave it be. He's entirely too much the gentleman to think of getting any of his own back, especially against a woman. Were you able to find any information for me, Hunter?"

"Some. I can tell you that Pamela Singer has never been charged with a crime, in America or Europe. I can tell you that she was born on June thirtieth, nineteen eighty. She was an only child and was raised in foster care after the death of her mother from a drug overdose when Pamela was five years old."

Dylan schooled himself against the wave of sympathy he sensed welling up inside him. Instead, he noted the fact of a broken home as likely one of the things about her that had appealed to his brother.

"Anything else? Anything a little more concrete that I can work with? What about a list of the men she's bilked?" He needed something to help him stay focused on the task at hand. Perhaps if he spoke to a few other of her victims, he'd be able to move Pamela out of the category of attractive female and into the slot of con artist.

Hunter's laugh sounded sardonic. "Older men, my young friend, aren't likely to step forward when taken to the cleaners by a sexy, younger woman."

"So what you're telling me is there's nothing."

"No, I'm not telling you that. I'm saying there's nothing on the record. I stumbled upon one piece of hearsay. It seems that a few years ago, Ms. Singer applied for a position with a New York conservatory—one that works with the leading galleries in the United States. The board nearly hired her, but the members changed their minds after a complaint lodged by a couple of their patrons—a brother and sister. Apparently, Ms. Singer preempted part of the sibling's inheritance when she had an affair with their uncle and manoeuvred herself into the old boy's will. And apparently, this wasn't the first time she'd canoodled with an older gent and walked away richer. My contact told me that the lady has earned an interesting moniker among some members of the art-patronage crowd. They call her *The Seductress*. But all of that, of course, is just gossip. You want facts, and I'm still working on it. When I get more, I'll send it via e-mail."

"Thanks, Hunter."

"No need. Good hunting. From what I've heard of her so far, you're going to need it."

Dylan slowly set the receiver down. Taking up his drink, he walked back to the windows and watched as night continued to fall on the City of Brotherly Love. Sipping from his glass, he decided not to think about the fact that he'd not told Hunter he'd already found Pamela Singer.

Or that he would be having dinner with her tomorrow night.

* * * *

"It's a good offer. The Heinrich Trust is well respected throughout the art world. And their headquarters is just north of the city." Pamela looked up to see what effect that last bit of news had and wasn't disappointed when both her sisters smiled.

They were all in Alba's spacious apartment, on her king-sized bed. This was a ritual that went back to the very beginning, to when they had become a family at the tender age of eleven. Friday nights they'd get into their pyjamas, scrounge food—the cookies and popcorn remained staples, but they'd switched the soda for wine—and just hang out together, doing their nails, their hair, or just plain gossiping. This was something Pamela had sorely missed in her years away.

"This city?" Alba asked.

"Yes." Pamela smiled in response to the excitement she saw in the other woman's eyes.

"And the other offer?" Twyla asked, looking at her with more contained enthusiasm.

It had always seemed to Pamela that, considering their chosen professions, her sisters had what should have been each other's personalities. Alba was easily affected, her moods up or down at the drop of a word. Twyla was always more schooled, her reactions always measured, her emotions held more closely to the vest. Yet Twyla was the one who used the persona of a social butterfly to gain access to the safes and vaults of the rich and bored, while Alba worked clandestinely for the government in a capacity she liked to call "trouble shooting."

"The other offer is from a small, privately owned gallery in the south of France. I'd be able to do the work in my own studio, which as you know, is part of my flat there."

"Do we have to tell you which one we want you to take?" Alba's question was delivered with what she was certain her sister considered a winsome smile.

"I know. But I have to think this through. Either offer would mean a long-term commitment. I have to be sure."

"What you need," Twyla said, ripping the top off a bag of chocolate-chip cookies, "is a good reason to stay stateside. Philly is close enough to New York that I can visit often."

"That is a good reason."

"Speaking of good reasons to stay," Alba interjected, "P.J. had sparkles in her eyes when she came back this afternoon. You know what that means!"

"The Louvre has offered her a position as their conservator-in-chief?"

Pamela laughed. Only her sisters had ever called her P.J.—she otherwise hated her middle name of Jane, and only her sisters had ever teased her. "I've missed the hell out of you guys." She reached for the bag of cookies Twyla was hogging. To Alba, she challenged, "I did *not* have sparkles in my eyes."

"You sure seemed happy when you got back from viewing that new exhibit this afternoon," Twyla agreed.

She was licking bits of chocolate from her fingers. It was, Pamela thought fondly, something that no one who knew her would ever expect to see. The woman could have been the poster girl for chic sophistication, and she was licking chocolate from her fingers like a kid.

"I'm always happy when I come back from a museum." That was just the right note of laid-back casual. Pamela flashed each of her sisters what she considered to be *her* most innocent smile. Now that she thought about it, by the time they'd hit thirteen, teasing each other about boys *had* become an integral part of this ritual.

"No, we've seen artsy-crafty happy before. This was a different kind of happy." Alba's tone was definite.

"This was man happy." Twyla made that pronouncement with equal surety.

"Man happy?"

Alba handed Pamela the bowl of popcorn and took the cookies in exchange. Then she picked up her glass of wine, downed a sizable gulp before continuing.

"Yes, man happy. I recognize the look because, up until a couple of months ago, it was the look I saw in the mirror every morning."

Pamela reached over and squeezed Alba's hand. She recalled how thrilled she'd been for her sister last year when Alba had called with the news that she'd met the man she was certain she was meant to spend the rest of her life with. And how heartbroken she'd been for her when she learned that this "perfect" man had dumped her.

"No, I'm not over him yet."

Twyla raised her glass. "May Patrick Jamieson roast in hell."

"I don't think Alba has reached the consign-him-to-hell point yet," Pamela said softly. "Even if we have."

Alba was shaking her head. "Not like you did so quickly with that good-for-nothing prick Andropolis. Not that I blame you one bit."

Pamela sighed and passed the popcorn to Twyla. Her wine glass was empty, so she had to stretch to reach the bottle that was on the floor. Once her glass was refilled with burgundy ambrosia, she sighed and decided to come clean with her sisters.

"That was different. I don't think I was all the way in love with him. I for sure never thought that he was *the one* destined to be mine."

"Oh, oh." Alba sat forward and set her glass down. "The way you said that can only mean that this man, whoever he is—"

"Yeah." Pamela sighed as she set her own glass down. "His name is Dylan Pierce, and he's with the Carstairs Hotel Chain. He's...I don't know how to describe him. T, D, and H, obviously. But the way I felt talking with him..." She looked from one sister to the other. "Do you recall the day we arrived at the Gibbons's? Three cast-off kids who had never met before, descending in one fell swoop on that sweet, middle-aged couple?"

"It was the most important day in my life to date," Twyla said quietly.

"I remember," Alba said.

"It felt as if we'd been born of the same blood and were *finally* reunited. As if we were meant to be sisters all along, and the universe came right because we finally were." Just speaking the words brought Pamela back to that day seventeen years before.

"That's how it was for you today, when you met Dylan Pierce? As if the universe had suddenly come right?" Alba's question, softly asked, spoke of understanding.

"Yeah. Only..."

"Only?"

Pamela shook her head. Twyla could come off so imperious when she looked at you that way. "Only after the way I fucked up with Dmitri, I don't know if I can trust my own judgement."

"Hey!" Alba's tone was suddenly fierce. "Don't you dare blame yourself for what happened with him. Not for one moment! Assholes like Dmitri Andropolis are masters at making people see them as they want to be seen. He played a role with you, and there was no way for you to have known what kind of a bastard he really was."

"Alba's right. You haven't let me investigate the scum-sucking prick, and you should. I'm awfully damn good at that. I'll bet you a million bucks he had an agenda all along where you were concerned that had *nothing* to do with romance."

There could be nothing better in life than having sisters who loved you unconditionally and were on your side no matter what.

Dmitri Andropolis had swept her off her feet nearly a year before. Handsome, sophisticated, and worldly, he had seemed completely enraptured by her in turn. She wondered if there wasn't something in her that kept searching for the father she'd never known by being attracted to older men.

Dmitri had been generous, constantly flattering her with flowers and small gifts, taking her to the best restaurants and theatres. Looking back, she supposed she should have wondered at the distance he seemed to keep between himself and his family, even if other men in her life had shown the same bent. He'd told her he was falling in love with her but had declined to even invite her to go with him when he'd gone home at Christmas. For her part, she'd wanted so badly to really be in love with him. She had come to care for him a great deal. She'd decided to work harder at their relationship, in fact, right after the holidays.

But when he'd returned, he'd been moody and argumentative. Pamela had been convinced the problem was hers, until their last date together, that weekend in London.

Dmitri had insisted on going to a casino, the Velvet Slipper. She'd been to casinos before and could take them or leave them. Dmitri had turned into another person altogether once the dice started to roll. Horrified, she watched as he lost toss after toss, as his impressive pile of chips got smaller and smaller. She pleaded with him to leave. He'd conceded, finally, seeming to be in a jovial enough mood.

Once outside the building, however, he'd turned on her, and with a viciousness that had frightened her, screamed invectives at her about keeping her place, backing up his verbal abuse with his hands, until she was on the ground and bleeding.

Even though he'd apologized immediately, as far as Pamela was concerned, from that moment on they'd been history.

Now she turned to her sisters.

"I love you both. Thanks for being in my corner. And thanks for thinking so highly of me. But the truth is, there were little red flags I should have noticed and didn't." The main one being, she thought now, that she hadn't been all the way in love with the man.

"Well then," Twyla said, snagging back the bag of cookies from Alba and stuffing one in her mouth. "You made an error in judgement. It happens. You didn't have that 'destiny' feeling with the SOB, and maybe that was the only red flag that really matters."

"Twyla's right. If you have that sense with Dylan Pierce, you should go for it. Take it slowly, one day at a time. But don't let one mistake rule your life or your choices."

It was the advice that she had desperately wanted to hear. But Pamela wondered if it really was the right advice for her.

Chapter 3

She wouldn't let him pick her up.

As he waited at the restaurant for his date to arrive, Dylan wondered what it meant. Was it because she didn't trust him or because she simply didn't want him to know where she was staying?

He'd bet the latter. She'd had long enough to check him out, to know that he wasn't an axe murderer, that he was who he claimed to be. He tried not to let the matter annoy him, but it did. His mother had raised him to be a gentleman on dates, and that meant picking his date up and delivering her back safely to her door.

Of course, Mother had never covered what the etiquette should be for hitting on a woman at a museum and dating her the next day, all with ulterior motives. It wasn't, he mused, an issue he'd likely discuss with her, either.

Motion caught his attention, and he looked up. One of the hosts approached, escorting Pamela. The moment he set eyes on her, every thought from the last few minutes lost importance.

Here was the woman who had stolen from his brother and caused Dmitri's disgrace among family and business associates, and the only thing Dylan could think was how much she appealed to him and how badly he wanted her.

What did that say about him? Or more importantly, what did that say about her? He was beginning to see why they called her *The Seductress*. Her sweetheart face and phenomenal eyes, smiling at him as they were now, could likely seduce any man out of anything she wanted.

"You look annoyed. Bad day?"

Dylan smiled, reminding himself that nothing would be gained if he pissed her off and she walked out. He only wished it was harder to push away his annoyance and caution.

"Sorry." He'd risen to his feet as she'd drawn near. Now he reached forward and brought her hand to his lips. "I was feeling annoyed because you insisted on meeting me here. I was wondering what my mother would think of my failure to behave like a proper gentleman."

Her laugh, a soft musical sound, actually had the effect of smoothing out his mood.

"Well, your mother would forgive you if she knew that I came here by taxi directly from a job interview."

When they were both seated, Dylan signalled to the waiter. The man came forward, displaying a bottle of merlot for Dylan's approval. Dylan nodded and indicated to the server that he could simply pour it out.

"Job interview? I thought you were on vacation." Actually, there was no thinking involved. He recalled everything she'd said the day before, and he knew for a fact she owned her flat in Paris.

"Oh, I am." Pamela paused for a moment and took a sip from her glass. Her smile told him she approved his selection. "But I've been offered a position with a private museum just north of the city. It would be a long-term assignment, as they have several paintings that need work. Since they contacted me and I'm here, I figured the least I could do was check it out. It would certainly make my sisters happy if I took it."

"Sisters?" Dylan was wondering what sort of game Pamela was playing. Hunter had told him she was an only child. If there was one thing Dylan had absolute faith in it was Hunter's research abilities.

"Mmm." She set her glass down as the waiter arrived.

Dylan continued to watch as the waiter opened a menu and gave it to her. He couldn't help but notice the kid—their waiter couldn't be more than twenty-two or three—could barely function, so taken was he with Pamela.

"The other offer I've received is from a small museum just outside of Paris. That one would allow me to bring the work to my studio, so I could essentially work at home, as I've been doing the last couple of years. But I honestly don't know if I want to stay in Europe any longer."

Dylan was beginning to wonder which way was up. The best course of action was to remember his goal. He certainly needed time to develop a solid relationship with Pamela. In order to exact revenge and recover the money, he needed to get close to her and stay close.

"Well, I for one hope you decide to accept the offer here. We've only just met. I want the opportunity to get to know you better."

He wished he could convince himself that the way his voice had just dipped and the sudden increase in his pulse rate when Pamela looked up from her menu and sent him that siren smile was part of the game plan.

But he couldn't lie to himself. Breaking their visual connection, he perused his menu. He wondered if Book Binder's served anything that would fortify his resistance to his dinner companion.

* * * *

Until she'd seen that smile and felt that husky male timbre wash over her, Pamela could have sworn there was something off with Dylan. Setting her menu down, she wondered at the serendipity of his having chosen Book Binder's for their date.

A famed restaurant in Philadelphia for longer than she'd been alive, Book Binder's had played a role in her earliest dreams and aspirations. When she'd been a budding teen, this restaurant had been in her mind as the epitome of grace, sophistication, and wealth. The newspapers carried stories of the rich and famous who dined within these walls. This restaurant had become a symbol of everything she longed to have when she grew up.

When she'd graduated college, Arthur Kensington, owner of the Kensington gallery where she worked, had brought her here for a celebratory dinner.

It had been a moment, and she'd been so touched that the old bear, as she'd called him, had thought to present her with such a gift. That dinner with him had been even more special than his bequest of the small gallery after his death.

She missed Arthur terribly.

"Your face is such a fascinating study. One moment you looked serene and the next very sad."

"I was just remembering the first time I ever dined here. I'd heard this place had closed, and that broke my heart. I came here for my college graduation dinner."

"It did close for renovations back in 2002. The kitchen, I'm told, hadn't seen any significant improvements since 1865. It turned out to need an extensive overhaul, which put the owners way over budget and behind schedule. When they reopened in 2005, it was a much smaller, more efficient Book Binder's. It used to take up three floors and serve eight hundred. But there are more restaurants per capita in this city now than there are in New York. Competition is fierce—too fierce to support such a large establishment."

Pamela tried to hide her astonishment. Dylan had rambled off that information as he perused the menu.

"I can see the shock on your face. The truth is out, so I might as well admit it. Yes, I'm a bit of a nerd."

"And you've just stumbled upon one truth about me. My sister Twyla chides me that I can't ever seem to hide my feelings."

"That's an interesting name, Twyla. Did your parents name all their daughters with a name ending in 'la'?"

Pamela blinked. *What an odd question.* "Ah, no. Actually, we don't have the same birth parents, the three of us. We decided we were sisters the day we met—when we all arrived at the same foster home at the same time."

"Oh. *Foster* sisters."

Why would Dylan look relieved at that? Or was she simply searching too hard for "red flags?" Whichever, she couldn't help the note of annoyance in her voice when she answered him. "No, as far as we're concerned, we're sisters, and that's that. You don't have to be of the same blood to be family."

The waiter came back at just that moment. Pamela ordered the red pepper bisque and the Surf and Turf. At Book Binder's that meant an eight-ounce filet mignon paired with a one-and-a-half-pound Maine lobster. It had been a long time since she'd had lobster. For good measure, since she was a bit ticked, she also ordered a side of creamed spinach. When she looked up, it was to encounter Dylan's tender expression.

He quickly gave his order to the waiter—President's salad as an appetizer and steak and crab cake for the entree. When they were alone again, he picked up her hand and squeezed it gently.

"I've offended you again. That's twice in as many days, and that's not good. I'm sorry. Really. Of course you're right. You don't have to be of the same blood to be family."

Pamela closed her eyes. *What the hell am I doing?* She knew the answer to that question, of course. She was painting Dylan with another man's colors. Had she not just affirmed to herself the night before that she was no man's victim? There was more than one way to let a bastard win, she realized as she opened her eyes and focused on Dylan. She had no business confusing the two men. If she continued in this vein, examining every little word, every gesture and expression of Dylan's, then she would, in fact, be handing tremendous power and a totally undeserved victory to that bastard Dmitri Andropolis.

"No, *I'm* sorry. I had a relationship go south on me recently, and I've let that failure come to dinner with us."

Dylan tilted his head slightly to the side. "Want to talk about it?"

Pamela had no doubt that his offer was sincere. In fact, she thought it might be a good thing to tell him about Dmitri, about every facet of that debacle from beginning to end. A man's perspective on another man's actions would probably be a good thing to have, maybe help her put that entire awful experience behind her for good. So maybe she'd take Dylan up on his offer.

But not tonight.

Tonight belonged to her, and to Dylan, and to that sense of...of *destiny* that had filled her yesterday when she'd turned her head at the museum and seen him for the first time. And Dmitri Andropolis belonged in the past.

"No, but thanks. Maybe I'll take a rain check on that conversation."

"All right, for now. But the offer stands. So tell me about Pamela Singer."

"There's not much to tell, really."

She sat back to allow the waiter to place the soup on the table in front of her.

"You're in Philadelphia on vacation from France, and you work with priceless pieces of art. Sounds as if there's a lot to tell."

"Not really. I'm just an ordinary woman. My part-time job after school at a small private gallery evolved into a lifetime calling."

"And you went to Europe because that's where most of the artistic masterpieces are?"

Pamela laughed. "That was a side benefit. I went to Europe because I wanted to see some of the world, and I ended up staying because I liked it there. What about you? You must travel a great deal, too."

"I do, and I've always considered that to be one of my biggest blessings. Having a mother from Athens and a father from San Francisco pretty much guaranteed I'd grow up more a citizen of the world than any one country."

"Where was home when you were a kid?"

"Well, Gran was a tough old bird—to the point of insisting on keeping her maiden name when she and Grandfather married—and nothing would do but that I be raised in California, right next door to her. However, my mother was an even tougher, if younger bird, and insisted on a compromise. I spent a lot of time with Gran, but mostly, home was in England."

"England?"

"Mm. When my parents met, Mother was living in England. She and my half brother were settled there. So Dad made the move from L.A. to London."

"So you have a half brother?"

"Yes. He's quite a bit older than I am, but he never minded having a baby brother. No sisters or other siblings, though. So you see, I do understand your feelings on family."

* * * *

He offered, but Pamela didn't want to go dancing, choosing instead to go for a walk.

They turned left from Book Binder's and headed toward the river. Walnut Street ended at Front, transforming into a pedestrian bridge over the expressway. It was a very nice bridge, brick and stone, lined with flowers and stone benches. This night there seemed to be so many people about, that a carnival like atmosphere prevailed. At the end of the bridge, Penn's Landing awaited any and all who wanted to enjoy the evening air and the river. The summer evening was warm and clear. She had no doubt she'd be able to see the stars if not for the ambient light of the walkway, as well as the two cities–Philadelphia and Camden, New Jersey, just across the river.

The breeze off the water was refreshing, and they stopped, turning their faces toward it. Music came from somewhere not too close, and Pamela thought it the perfect accompaniment to the sound of the gently lapping wake of boats. They walked around the Sea Port Museum, the red brick smooth underfoot.

Laughter, lights, and children playing all worked together to ease her stress. She put away all the errant whimpers from the past that had dared to intrude on this evening. When Dylan reached for her hand, she gave it. She felt entirely comfortable in his company. "There's something about the carnival-like atmosphere in places like this that is so joyous. It just draws me," she said, pausing to watch the crowds yet again.

"There is, yes. The music and happy faces all around us and the scent of grilled meat and something sweet carried on the breeze, brushed with a lightness of spirit only found in the midst of a crowd of vacationers."

Dylan's description was exactly right. She couldn't help but turn to him at that moment. They were surrounded by people, and yet when her gaze met his, everyone else seemed to simply disappear. She didn't have to ask if he felt the same way. The heat in his eyes said it all. The pull irresistible, Pamela stretched, forward and up, unable to do anything else. He met her halfway.

His lips were warm on hers, soft and seeking, a perfect fit. His flavor drenched her, the heat of his body warmed her when she'd not even known she'd been chilled. Her right hand reached up, caressed his cheek.

He angled his head, and she had more of him, more of his taste and his heat. Her tongue caressed, lapped and licked every bit of his mouth, and her arousal soared. *Better than chocolate.* Then her mind simply turned all focus on her body and what this delicious man made her feel.

When he gathered her in closer, she wound her arms around his neck and held on. The ground seemed to drop away from beneath her feet. Lust and longing wound through her, golden rivers that took her deep. Dylan's tongue in her mouth caressed and claimed, and she found surrender a ripe fruit within, eager to be picked and plundered by this man and no other. Moving her hips to try and capture the rising ridge of his erection against her mons, a frantic yearning erupted. She needed his flesh rubbing against hers, his cock buried deep inside her. This was crazy, insane, unlike anything she'd ever experienced in her entire life. She was cautious by nature, had never rushed headlong into the physical side of a relationship

The urge to mate with this man overpowered every thought, every reason, and every caution.

His hands framed her face, but even when he weaned his lips from hers, he continued to sip at her cheeks, her eyes, while his thumbs stroked her face and his plea caressed her skin.

"Come upstairs with me, baby."

Chapter 4

Pamela stepped back from the precipice. Feeling light-headed and dazed, she blinked when Dylan's hands slid to her arms and held her anchored even as his words washed through her.

"Up?" She would have sworn she was already "up" as high as it was humanly possible for her to go. Dylan's smile simply melted her. The flick of his gaze over his shoulder brought her focus away from passion and back to her surroundings.

Rising high above them, shimmering in light and awash in color, the Philadelphia Riverfront Carstairs Hotel stood in command of the Landing, the river, and the entire area. *Ah, yes.* This was Dylan's hotel.

"Yes, come up with me. Please. I'll...make us some coffee."

His hands began to caress her arms, up and down, a silky, sensuous continuation of their kiss. His touch was powerful. Soothing, arousing, and reaching deep into her soul, it made everything that had been off-kilter within her, right.

"It isn't coffee either of us wants."

Her response evaporated his smile, leaving him with a hungry, haunted look she didn't understand.

"It isn't, no. And it's probably very foolish on both our parts to take this next step so soon, to rush headlong into sex. Except I think it's going to be a hell of a lot more than just sex, and I truly believe if we turn back from this now, it'll prove to be something we'll both regret for the rest of our lives."

"A sense of destiny?" Despite the attempted levity in her tone, she was very serious.

"Yes, damn it. And to be honest, all things considered, that scares the hell out of me."

She'd think about the enigma of his statement later. Her plan had been to dismiss the sense of inevitability she felt the first moment she set eyes on Dylan Pierce. The feeling had seemed real, just as she'd told her sisters. But, also as she'd told her sisters, she couldn't trust her own judgement. Not after Dmitri.

Knowing Dylan felt the same way tossed that plan right out the window. What were the chances that he'd admit to something that could be considered so levelling for a man if it wasn't the truth? Pamela didn't know what was happening between them, but she'd worry about that later. Such urgency raced through her veins she wondered if she would survive it. In the face of these emotions and the soul-deep belief that this was meant to be, that *they* were meant to be, she could say only one thing.

"All right, yes. I'll come up."

* * * *

His hands were shaking.

Dylan couldn't remember if he'd ever before wanted a woman so badly that his hands shook. He knew she saw it, too, as he inserted the key into the lock. He didn't care about that. He didn't care that this was the woman who had brought his brother to ruin, either. There was only one thing he cared about: getting his hands on Pamela Singer as quickly as possible. He turned to her the moment the door closed behind them.

"Come here."

He didn't give her a chance to respond. He seized on her arms and pulled her up and into his kiss.

When he'd tasted her for the first time downstairs, he'd thought— he'd hoped—that sense of destiny, that taste of ambrosia had been a trick of the summer night, the lights, and the joie de vivre of the crowd that had surrounded them.

Heaven. How could she taste like heaven, feel better than every wet dream he'd ever had? Her heat seeped into him, and he pulled her closer, pressing her female curves against his hard and hungry body. Her arms went around his neck as his hands splayed across her bottom, bringing her to his erection.

Drinking her in, he lifted her off her feet, grunting when she wrapped her legs around him.

He'd only been in residence in this penthouse a week, but he found the bedroom without taking his lips from hers. Her tongue danced with his, their flavors mixing in a concoction more potent than a wizard's potion. Soft and sweet, hot and heady, Dylan felt himself succumb completely to her spell. Not wanting to let her go even for a moment, he fell with her to the bed.

He sought the flavor of her cheeks, her neck, and reveled in her touch, so anxious against his scalp. Pamela was devouring him in turn, and that thrilled him beyond measure. *No other woman before her has mattered*. The image flashed of a violent sea, of his being lured to rocky ruin on the shore of some forgotten, mythical island. Then the image was gone, forced out by his need for her and his own conscious choice.

He looked down at her while he raced to catch his breath. Her eyes were clouded with passion, edged with confusion.

"I don't usually—"

Stroking a finger lightly across her mouth, he silenced her. He didn't want her to speak, didn't want a call to reason, not for either of them. He knew he was on dangerous ground, knew he should get up, walk away, hell, walk all the way back to Greece. But he couldn't.

He wouldn't.

"I know you don't usually. Neither do I. Let's not talk. Let's just feel."

For one instant, he thought she would refuse him. He'd let her go, of course. He wasn't an animal. But then her expression cleared, and she stroked his face gently.

A loving gesture, not a lustful one. He realized that, for Pamela, no matter what else there was to her, having sex would never be a matter of whim, of lust only.

He refused to think what more it could be. With fingers that had calmed, he began to open her blouse.

Creamy flesh and white lace enticed him. Compelled, he set his mouth on her, sampling her collarbone, her throat, as his busy fingers finished their task. Lifting her, he swept the silky fabric from her, leaving only her bra covering her plump breasts. He felt his smile spread as he took in the front closure on the garment. His mouth set about freeing her.

Her groan of arousal spurred him on, and he drew a pebbled nipple even deeper into his mouth. Her hands tugged at his clothing. He lifted up from her slightly.

Pamela's hands were quick and competent as they loosened his tie and then his buttons. The moment the last one opened, he whipped off his shirt, not caring that the fine linen fell to the floor in a heap. The touch of her hands on his chest, her fingers splaying to caress and grip, shot straight to his groin.

Her arms crept up to twine around his neck. He shook his head. Reaching down, he slipped the button on her trousers from its mooring and pulled the zipper down. Their hands worked together quickly to get the clothes off.

The dark hair covering her intimate flesh was the same delectable shade as the rest of her hair and promised to be just as soft. Unable to resist, he stroked her gently, his touch a light and fleeting caress. He chuckled when she bowed off the bed.

Every bit of humor left him when she reached out and returned the intimacy, her hand pressing against the ridge covered by his pants. It took him only moments to shed the rest of his clothes. He reached into the drawer of his bedside table, not taking his eyes from her, and grabbed a tiny foil packet. Tearing it open with his teeth, he pulled out the condom, rolled it on, and covered her.

"Open for me, baby."

Her legs spread for him, and he had one instant to appreciate the texture of her hot, moist folds against the head of his penis. Then he plunged.

* * * *

Oh, God. Pamela melted as Dylan thrust into her, as his hard shaft sank straight to her cervix. Leaving her no time to draw breath, her orgasm erupted from that impact, delicious and shivery and all-consuming. Pushing her hips hard and fast, she tried to draw out the cataclysm. Dylan's rhythm raced, and sweat beaded on his body. She wrapped herself around him, held on, and enticed by his scent, by the man-musk that drew her, stretched up and sampled him with her tongue. Salty, primal, she imagined herself absorbing him completely, imagined that there was not one spot of her that didn't now contain him as a basic essence of her being.

"*More!*"

His growl could have been a command, but she was beyond caring. Bowing up further, she ground her hips, managing to rub her clit against his groin, the coarse hair stimulating a second orgasm before the first had fully ebbed. She felt his cock quiver and pulse inside her. Tidal waves of rapture washed everything else away, until there was nothing in the world but the two of them, groaning in erotic bliss.

Striving for breath, she let her arms slide off him as orgasmic aftershocks rippled through her. Her nipples had gone painfully stiff and hard, a rare personal affectation that signaled a particularly powerful climax.

"*Mother of God*." His words puffed hot, moist breath on her neck. She was awfully glad that Dylan seemed to be as wrecked as she was.

"I think you better call the front desk and make sure your hotel is still standing."

"Can't move," he whispered in her ear and then belied that by thrusting slightly. He was still semi-hard within her, and she smiled.

"Can too. You just did."

"Mmm. That I can manage. Don't want to overreach, so I think I'll just limit myself to that for the next few days. At least until the debris from that earthquake clears."

"Few days? You'll kill us both."

"You have a point. Ok. Scratch the few days. How about if we start with just tonight, then? Will you stay the night?"

His warmth surrounded her, and the sensation of him still deep within her sent wonderful little flicks of pleasure all through her. Her inner muscles convulsed, squeezing him, and she was immediately rewarded by his renewing vigor.

"I'll stay."

She might regret the decision; hell, she might regret the whole damn night. The morning would be soon enough to worry about consequences.

* * * *

"We have a problem requiring immediate attention."

As those disembodied words echoed in the quiet room, Peter Abbot had the definite feeling that his life was about to go for a shit.

He'd had that feeling since receiving the e-mail directing him to this fifth-floor Paris hotel room this morning. They generally took their meetings—when meeting was required—in innocuous hotel rooms.

Peter's thoughts leapt back to the beginning. It had all begun as a lark. Peter and his best friend Dmitri Andropolis, bored one summer, had decided upon the ultimate hobby: larceny. Both the sons of wealthy families, they'd thought playing at crime not only marvelous fun but an excellent way to snub their noses at their entire social class. The first few times Peter had stood and listened sympathetically as friends of his father lamented the theft of some trinket—knowing he'd had a hand in stealing the thing—had been the biggest high of his life. After all, it was just stuff; the old geezers had been insured, and so nobody got hurt.

Over time, they'd taken three others into their game. Gradually, though, the fun had worn off. Recently, he'd been regretting his youthful transgressions. Older now, he looked back on his past with a different perspective. He'd committed criminal acts. Poised to take over the family business, thinking of getting married, the truth of his past was an uncomfortable one, indeed. This latest fiasco made it even more so.

The plan had been hatched by Andropolis. Since the bulk of the work was on him and another of their group, Peter hadn't batted an eye. Even so, he'd begun to search for a way to get out of this trap he'd managed to work himself into.

However, the plan that had begun as a "sure thing" had quickly fallen apart, thanks to the growing instability of his oldest friend.

His attention focused on the speaker phone sitting in the middle of the small, round table.

"I'm afraid Andropolis has become a serious liability."

The tone booked no argument. Peter Abbot took a moment to survey his colleagues. Timmy Sykes twitched in his chair, but that was normal for the second-story man. The short, wiry Liverpuglian had once confided to Peter that he saw no need for meetings. "Like meself was some bloody nabob or such," he'd scoffed. The other man taking up space at the table was Timmy's polar opposite in every respect. Tall, dapper, but with a lethal edge to him, Jeremy Irons was the group's forger and, Peter thought, their most dangerous member. "'e was destined to be a forger. Not even 'is name is original," Timmy had once said. But not within Jer's hearing, of course. Street-savvy Timmy knew to steer clear of the other man.

"He's more than a liability," Irons said now, his New York accent just barely discernable. "This is why I wanted us to meet. We have a more serious problem than we thought."

"There's something else, then?" the telephone voice asked.

The identity of the fourth member of the group was known only to Andropolis, who'd never revealed the man's name. Referred to by the rest of them as simply "The Banker," his role was organizational, as well as providing the group whatever raw materials were needed to get the job done. His voice was always disguised by a mechanical synthesizer, a rather paranoid precaution, Peter thought. Since none of them knew the man, they were unlikely to ever recognize him should they meet.

But The Banker knew each one of them. Until recently, that fact hadn't bothered Peter at all.

Peter turned his attention back to the meeting. He was very aware that Jeremy was taking his time, drawing out the drama.

"While I was—persuading—Dmitri to come up with that half million in compensation for the job he fucked up, he told me the woman knows the entire setup. Not only what we'd planned to do, but also who each of us is." He flashed a smile that made Peter's blood run cold before focusing his gaze on the speaker phone. "Every last one of us, including you, banker."

"I see."

The Banker's voice had become even more remote, if that was possible. It took everything he had for Peter to keep his tone blasé. "It's been weeks. If what you say is true, why haven't we all had the constabulary knocking on our doors?" he asked.

"Ms. Singer is hardly above reproach, herself. I'm digging deeper into her past. It's highly unlikely that she would ever turn any information she came into over to the police," The Banker said.

"Well then? She's just a skirt."

Timmy's comment was dismissive, uncharacteristically so. In that moment, Peter realized he wasn't the only person in the group having grave misgivings about the wisdom of this association.

"There's nothing to stop her from using her information for profit, though. That's exactly what I would do in her place." Irons's tone was clipped.

"Exactly. Not the cops, but the same end. We'd be betrayed, and either in prison or at the bottom of some ocean somewhere."

"The truth is, none of us are safe." That assertion by Irons hit home.

Peter frowned. He found himself in the position of agreeing with both of his colleagues. If Pamela Singer *did* know about them, they weren't any of them safe.

The truth was a cold, hard reality. To the right person, the information she had about them would be worth a small fortune. And if the wrong people found out about this little group, then the world Peter wanted for himself would disintegrate before he even had the chance to fashion it.

"There is, in fact, only one way we can all be safe. If Ms. Singer ceases to exist, so does any threat to us." As The Banker's words echoed in the room, Peter felt the walls closing in around him.

"There's still Dmitri. He's becoming more out of control as time goes on," Irons said.

"I'll see to Andropolis. Peter, you among us are the most well acquainted with The Provider. I'll arrange the transaction from here. You be our liaison with the man."

Very aware of Irons's narrow-eyed scrutiny, Peter schooled his expression, revealing nothing of what he really felt.

"Consider it done. I'm scheduled to fly back to London tomorrow afternoon. I'll pay him a visit tomorrow night."

Seeing the look of cold satisfaction in Irons's eyes reaffirmed his worst fears. The Banker had claimed that they'd all be safe only once

Pamela Singer had been eliminated. But there'd been something in Jeremy's eyes that told him she was far from the only threat he faced.

For now, he'd fooled them and even bought himself some time. Time he would use to try and find a way to get out from under the mess he'd made.

Chapter 5

"Sister of mine, you look happy enough for the both of us."

Pamela shot Alba a quick grin and then turned her attention back to the matter at hand, shopping. Or, specifically, helping Alba shop for a biker-chick wardrobe.

The secondhand store was in a less affluent area of the city. Here, buildings were slowly falling to ruin, and bits of refuse had been allowed to pile up in corners and alleyways. Pamela had visited several large cities both in North America and Europe, and in this aspect, they were all the same. Some areas were modern, clean, and wealthy. And others were run down, with urban decay having gotten more than a toehold.

"Are you suffering from coital envy?" Pamela asked, eliciting a chuckle from her sister.

"No, Bob and I are doing just fine, thank you."

Pamela leaned closer so she wouldn't be overheard. "Well, there are advantages to having a battery-operated boyfriend, I suppose. Though thinking hard, none come to mind at the moment."

"I've really missed you," Alba returned when she'd stopped laughing. "I've missed both you and Twyla. It's just too bad that I have to take this assignment now, when you're both visiting."

"You do interesting work," Pamela offered as she held up a scruffy leather jacket. "And since you said this would take only a few days, we'll still be here when you're done."

Her sister tried on the jacket, grinning when it fit perfectly.

"The work isn't that interesting," Alba confided. "But getting to play dress-up is."

There was more to it than her words revealed. Pamela understood that, just as she saw that the career Alba had embarked upon just out of college was wearing on her. Her next words confirmed it.

"Do you know what the life span is for someone in my profession? Ten years. I'm beginning to understand why."

"Honey, if it's that bad, quit."

Alba's expression turned uncharacteristically somber. "I can't just up and quit. I have to have a plan. Sure, they say you can let go. But try finding anyone who has. Anyone alive, that is."

A cold chill coursed down Pamela's spine. It wouldn't serve any purpose to remind her sister that both she and Twyla had begged her not to take the job the government recruiter offered all those years ago. Alba, bless her, had been far too patriotic to say no at the time.

"Then maybe you should consider getting yourself a plan."

"I'm working on it. I figure two more years. I can keep it up for that long." She exhaled deeply, fluffing the hair that hung down from her forehead. Then she flashed a big smile. "Enough about me. Now tell me about Mr. Tall, Dark, and Horny."

Pamela had always been good at taking cues from Alba. She knew her sister wouldn't be pushed on anything, and that she'd do whatever it was she'd decide to do in her own good time.

Humoring her, she smiled and asked, "What do you want to know?"

"Ooh, sex by proxy. Yummy. I want every salacious detail."

"Well, you're not going to get them." Of course, she knew Alba was kidding. And she knew what her sister really wanted to know.

"This past week has been...unbelievable." She couldn't help the way her voice went soft when she was speaking about Dylan Pierce. "No matter where we go or what we're doing, we click. I've never felt this sense of simpatico with a man before. And yet—" And yet, she thought. Because it was her sister she was talking to, she let the thoughts, the doubts, fully form. "There are moments, just funny little isolated moments, when I think there's something else going on with us—with him. I'll turn to Dylan and see a look in his eyes, as if he's trying to examine me under a microscope. As if he doesn't believe a word I say. Just flashes, and then they're gone."

"Are those moments really there, or are you still reading too much into every nuance?"

Pamela didn't regret telling her sisters about her feelings during that first dinner date with Dylan. They had both agreed that she could very well be substituting one man for the other.

"I don't know."

"My advice? You've been seeing each other every day since the day you met last week. Maybe what you need is a couple of days off from each other. Days where you don't see him at all. Then come back to this relationship with a fresh attitude."

It was good advice, Pamela thought as she followed her sister through the secondhand store. She just wasn't certain she could follow it.

* * * *

He'd given himself a firm lecture before leaving his office to meet Pamela for lunch. And, as usual, the words and sense of it evaporated the moment he saw her waiting for him. Of course, he couldn't keep his hands off her. Couldn't resist tasting her just a tiny bit the moment he'd closed the distance between them.

He'd meant to keep the kiss light and the embrace casual, but quickly lost himself in her. He nearly growled when she stepped back. "Sorry. I always get carried away."

"I've noticed. But we're standing in the lobby of your hotel, and the staff, like staff everywhere, probably love to gossip."

Dylan looked around but could see no one watching them, particularly. She was right, of course. He thought to leave it alone as he began to lead her toward the restaurant that was tucked away in the corner of the ground-floor lobby. His mouth betrayed him.

"That bothers you? People seeing us together?"

"No. I was actually thinking of you and your position here."

He caught the cooling of her tone and cursed himself. He'd better learn to stop jumping to conclusions with Pamela—at least out loud. The look she was giving him was one he'd seen on her face a few times in the last week, usually just after he'd jammed his foot into his big mouth.

The problem, of course, was that the more time he spent with Pamela Singer the more trouble he was having casting her in the role of destructive siren. The woman he was coming to know simply didn't come off as a cold, calculating, money-grubbing gold digger.

But to be perfectly honest, he hadn't given her any opportunity to show that side of herself. Maybe she was on vacation in more ways than one. As the hostess escorted them to a table by the window overlooking the river, Dylan decided it was time to do what he'd set out to do a few weeks ago. It was time to bait a trap.

"I haven't asked, as I've been trying to be patient, but the suspense is killing me. Have you decided whether or not you're going to accept the job with the Heinrich Trust?"

He'd caught her off guard with his question. He was already getting to know her facial expressions, and he didn't think he'd ever known a woman whose emotions revealed themselves so clearly in her eyes. Or so it seemed.

"No, I've not decided yet. When they made the offer last Wednesday, I told them I'd like a couple of weeks to think about it. As they're not in a hurry, they agreed to hold the position open, giving me the time."

He reached forward, picked up her hand, and kissed it. "I want you to stay in Philadelphia."

"Do you?"

The smile she sent him attacked the puny emotional defenses he had against her. "Yes. Enough to sweeten the deal."

She tilted her head to the side. "What did you have in mind?"

"I'll authorize a substantial donation to the trust, with the proviso they add two-thirds of it to the stipend they're offering you."

She pulled her hand back slowly, and although her smile remained in place, the chill that entered her eyes wasn't what he'd expected to see.

"How efficient. You can pay for sex and get a tax write-off at the same time."

"What? No!" Although that was exactly what he was implying, hearing her speak the words aloud changed everything, made his suggestion sound dirty, somehow.

"Well, I can guarantee you that's how it'll look to them. And that's how it would feel to me."

She'd closed her menu and set it aside. Dylan realized if he didn't do something fast, she was going to walk out on him.

"I keep saying the wrong things to you. I didn't mean it like that. Honest to God, Pamela. I just thought that nonprofit organizations don't usually have much of a budget, so whatever they're offering can't be a lot of money. And you'd have to, I don't know, close up your flat in Paris, move. Taking the position here could turn out to be an expensive proposition for you."

"It would be, yes. But that isn't any of your concern."

Reaching across the table, he took her hand in his. He tried to dismiss the sense of real panic that was running through him. He was worried because his mission was in danger of ending before he'd succeeded, that's all. Time to pour on some of the charm his mother always claimed he had too much of. "I just want you to stay here, Pamela. I'm sorry if my suggestion offended you. That's the last thing I wanted to do. I just found you. I don't want you to leave."

"If you donate that sum—even if you do it anonymously—I'll turn down the offer and return home next month, as I'd originally planned."

"All right, I won't. Please, accept my apology." In the face of her apparent implacability, it was the only thing he could say. He couldn't read her expression in the moments that followed, and that worried him even as it reinforced the whisper of suspicion he still felt about her. She could disguise her feelings when she wanted to.

"All right. I accept your apology."

"Thank you. Now, let's have lunch."

He only relaxed when she picked up her menu once more. But something about the edge she'd just shown him seemed out of character with the woman he'd come to know. It was enough, he reasoned against his growing guilty conscience, to justify his suspicions and his actions.

He'd offered her cash, and she'd turned him down. Even as he gave the waitress his order, another plan was forming. Maybe Pamela didn't want to show her true colors to him. But he was willing to bet she might to a mark who was more in line with her usual preferences. She liked her "men" older, more sophisticated, and he had the perfect candidate in mind.

* * * *

Her sister was right. She needed space from that man.

This was why she'd declined his offer of dinner last night and why she'd told him she was going to be busy all day, today.

Of course, she hadn't made any plans. But that was never a problem. Long before she'd found herself in her last foster home and with sisters, she'd learned the art of amusing herself and avoiding boredom. She didn't need the company of someone else in order to enjoy the treat of an outdoor café.

As she sat, absorbing the fresh air and enjoying her latte, she thought back to yesterday's lunch. It seemed incredible to her Dylan had no idea how his "offer" would sound. What was it about men that made them so damned dense? In her experience, it was a condition not restricted to the younger of the species, either. Most men could be counted on to put their foot in it from time to time, where women were concerned.

"You put me in mind of a painting—Valkyrie, beautiful and fierce, come to claim lost souls for Odin! That wonderful painting was in the Kunsthal Museum in Rotterdam when I was there last year."

The gentleman who'd spoken was dressed nattily in grey Armani, his dark brown eyes twinkling beneath eyebrows that were as snowy white as the hair on his head and the beard on his chin. A cane was hooked on his wrist, and his hands held a tray bearing a coffee cup and a plate with a delectable-looking pastry. There was something so engaging about his smile she couldn't hold back her own.

"I think I was feeling like one for a moment."

"Probably some scoundrel of a man, no doubt, put that edge of remoteness in your eyes. Young pups today have absolutely no sense about them when it comes to women. They're all ego and hot air, full of themselves and their importance in the universe—as they see it. A man doesn't reach a proper understanding of what life's all about—or how to properly treat a beautiful woman—until he's crossed the half-century mark."

He reminded her of Arthur Kensington. Though not nearly as rotund as her late mentor, he had the same professorial demeanor. She'd thought of Arthur during her first date with Dylan, and her mind had touched on him off and on since then.

"Would you like to join me?"

"Ah, you're being kind to this old man. Thank you, I will."

"I'd hardly call you old."

"My dear young woman, I'll never see sixty again."

The whispered confidence was accompanied by twinkling eyes and an almost cherubic grin. She'd bet that in his younger days this gentleman had been hell on wheels.

He could still be, for all of that.

Once he was seated, he removed his cup and the dessert plate from his tray, setting the tray aside.

"I've become a creature of habit. I stop at this café every week at this time. I don't believe I've seen you here before."

"No, I just discovered it today, so it's my first time." The early afternoon sun and the light breeze put Pamela in mind of any number of sidewalk cafés she'd visited in Paris, Marseille, and Cannes over the past couple of years. The only difference she could see was the language floating in the air.

"Just the café, or the city as well?" he asked.

"The café. I grew up in Philadelphia, though I'm visiting at the moment."

"I'm only just relocated myself, from New York. Eric Llewellyn."

"Pamela Singer. It's nice to meet you, Mr. Llewellyn." She offered him her hand and felt her heart melt just a little when he raised it to his lips and kissed it.

"Please call me Eric. I'm delighted you chose this café today. It's been a while since I've spent time with a beautiful woman."

"Now it's you who are being too kind."

"Not at all." He took a sip of his coffee then set the cup down. "There's an air about this city, a hint of grace and sophistication that you don't find in that metropolis to the east that I've just left. The tenor of life is more genteel here." He sat back and looked at her.

One thing about older men, Pamela thought as she felt herself becoming aware of this gentleman's scrutiny, they weren't embarrassed to look their fill and let you know that's exactly what they were doing.

"I hope you won't be offended, Ms. Singer, but I've always considered myself a man of superior perception and exquisite tastes. You appear to be as graceful and sophisticated as this city. Looking at you, I could almost believe you European."

Pamela smiled. "I'm not at all offended, Eric."

Pamela knew when a man was flirting with her. He was handsome, no question about it, and more in line with her usual tastes than Dylan. "As I've lived in France for a number of years, it's understandable that you'd think me European. There is a distinct difference in cultures, isn't there?"

"Indeed. I find Europeans far more reasonable about so many things...the pace of life, the importance of good food, good wine...and of course, their attitude toward sex."

No doubt about it, Eric Llewellyn had just come on to her. This was a dance familiar to her, a dance as old as time.

Pamela smiled, already anticipating the next step.

Chapter 6

The knock on the door caught Dylan unawares. He wasn't expecting anyone. Looking through the security viewer, he identified his surprise visitor and promptly opened the door.

"I didn't expect to see you this evening." He stepped back, allowing Pamela into his suite.

Not expecting to see her was an understatement. As he'd eaten a solitary dinner delivered by room service, he'd been driving himself crazy thinking about what it was she would likely be doing with her time tonight. It didn't matter that he'd been the one to engineer her meeting with Eric. He hated the thought of her with his old friend. So he'd tried his best to keep his attention focused elsewhere. He'd tried to immerse himself in work—he may have been in Philadelphia on a personal quest of vengeance, but he was still an executive in his grandmother's company. And one of his father's, too, come to that.

Then Pamela turned to face him, and he realized how his words of greeting just now had sounded. The look of hurt that brushed her face found an answering pang in his gut.

"I'm sorry. I should have called first," she said. Turning, she took one step toward the door.

"No."

To hell with it. He pulled her into his arms, his mouth fastening on hers, and plundered. Anger and frustration evaporated as he wrapped his arms around her and felt hers surround him. His tongue caressed and danced with hers, and her flavor filled and soothed him. One kiss was never enough, could never be enough. He wanted more. He wanted all.

The phone rang.

Pamela stepped back, her hand caressing his face lightly. "You should get that. I'll wait."

He watched her walk over to the windows as he reached for the phone. He was determined to make this the shortest conversation in history.

"Pierce."

"Well, my friend, I gave it my best shot. I poured on the charm, and for a while there I thought I was going to succeed."

Dylan's eyes stayed on Pamela, taking in the easy way she enjoyed the view from the expansive glass balcony doors as his old friend's voice filled his ear and his head. *Shit, this could be tricky.*

"Is that right?"

"Ah, I hear caution in your tone. Might I surmise that the beautiful Ms. Singer is there with you now?"

"You may." Dylan flashed a grin when Pamela turned for a moment to look at him. Thank God Eric was an intelligent man. "Thank you for calling. If that's all?"

"Just one more thing. She told me she was seeing someone and that it was a fairly new relationship, or otherwise she'd have taken me up on my offer. Take a word of advice from an old man. Don't throw away a golden opportunity."

"I'll certainly consider that. Thank you for taking the time to call. Good-bye."

Dylan replaced the receiver and walked over to the woman who had become far more important to him than he'd ever dreamed possible.

"Now, where were we?" he asked, reaching for her.

Pamela shook her head slowly. "Where we've been entirely too often since we met. I didn't come here for that tonight."

Dylan felt his gut clench. He nearly let his nerves come through in his voice. Perhaps it was his conscience that was telling him he deserved to have her walk away from him now. He really didn't think he could tell the difference between right and wrong in this situation any longer. At the last moment, he tramped down the edge that wanted to bleed into his words.

"No? Why did you come here, then?"

If he didn't know better, he'd have sworn that Pamela was actually nervous. Folding his arms, he leaned against the sturdy glass of the balcony doors, pasted an expectant expression on his face, and waited.

"Since our first evening out, I've been…I guess you could say I've been punishing you for another man's crimes."

"Ah, yes. The relationship that so recently went wrong. You mentioned it at *Book Binder's*. My offer to listen still stands. Or…are you perhaps discovering that you're still in love with the guy?" And wouldn't *that* be a kick in the ass? In the next instant, he realized that wasn't what Pamela was saying. The relief that swept him left him even more confused than he had been.

"No. There's absolutely no chance of that. After he…well, after, I realized that I hadn't cared for him as much as I'd thought I had. Not only that, but I kicked myself for having allowed the relationship to progress as far as it had. The thing is, I've spent entirely too much time allowing what happened months ago to color what's happening now. I decided yesterday at lunch, when I nearly jumped down your throat, that what we needed was a break from each other. But now I realize that what *I* need is to consign the past *to* the past. And because that's what I have to do, I'll say no, thanks, to your offer to listen. And I'll also say I'm sorry. I'm sorry I've treated you, and us, the way I have."

Dylan's mind was looking for hidden meanings in Pamela's words, while his body just wanted to haul her close and hold her tight. As for his heart, he wasn't entirely certain where that fickle creature weighed in on either the situation or the woman.

Without thinking further, he straightened up and took one step closer. "You've got nothing to apologize for, Pamela. And frankly, I don't blame you one bit for taking exception to some of the things I've said since we met." He couldn't stop from reaching out, setting his hands on her arms and slowly drawing her closer. *His body was winning, it seemed.* "I don't think I can recall a time when I've been quite so prone to foot-in-mouth disease. Maybe the problem is that you matter. You matter very much on several different levels, and I don't quite know how to deal with that." *That, at least, was the complete, unvarnished truth.*

"He was wrong."

The non sequitur found him tilting his head just slightly. "Who was wrong?"

"An older gentleman I met today. He said younger men didn't know how to handle women properly. But you're doing just fine."

"Am I?"

"Mmm." She took a step closer, eliminating the distance between them. "I'd say so. Actually, he was a very nice man and made me a very interesting offer."

"Do I want to hear about this offer?"

Pamela's smile warmed him straight to his bones. "He was a perfect gentleman, Dylan. And I did turn him down. As a matter of fact, I told him I was involved with someone else."

"Good." So many conflicting thoughts and feelings, Dylan mused, needed to be put to bed. *And they aren't the only things that need to go to bed.* Framing her face with his hands, he lowered his lips to hers. Her taste had already become necessary to his existence, her flavor a part of him. Closing his arms around her, he lifted her then broke their kiss.

"I want to be inside you. Any objections?"

The way she wrapped herself around him put him in mind of a surrender, though he'd never met a more self-assured woman in his life. When she nuzzled his neck, everything inside him warmed. And when she whispered in his ear, "not a one," he could only wonder if he could get them horizontal, and naked, soon enough.

* * * *

Smoke hung blue and heavy in the air. The voices of men rising and falling with the rhythm of conversation resembled an odd sort of breathing. The scent of beer and cigarettes consumed every bit of space. Here a man could carouse with friends, watch the latest football match on the Telly, or silently slide into his cups with no one paying so much as a never-mind. Here men could and did hide from spouses, employers, loan sharks, and life. If only a man could become someone else between rounds, then this pub in a dingy part of London could be certified as heaven.

Timmy Sykes shook his head, wondering where that whimsical thought had come from. If ever there was a time for cold, hard thinking, it was now.

He was afraid for his life and not ashamed to admit it to himself. He'd never particularly liked the entire group he'd hitched himself to years before. That Greek, Andropolis, was all right. Though he knew the man capable of putting on airs, he'd never treated Timmy with anything but kindness and respect. Peter wasn't too bad, either, though if they happened to cross paths in town here, that nabob was as likely to treat him as a complete stranger as not. *Couldn't hold that against the bloke, really*. A man had to take care of himself and his own. What you did out and about was one thing. What came home to roost on your doorstep quite another.

But those other two of his "partners in crime" were pure vipers. Irons would as soon run a blade across your throat as nod hello to you, and with just about as much emotion, too. As for the one they all called "The Banker"—well, it was never a good thing to be in larceny with a man who knew everything about you while keeping his own hows and whys a secret.

Timmy pulled a fifty-pence piece out of his pocket and let it walk through his fingers as he thought. There'd be no work coming from the group until that unknown banker gave the all clear, and who in God's name knew when that would be? Timmy had some other options, of course. A bloke had to have his options. But what had gone down a few days ago in Paris had left him with a distinctly uneasy feeling.

Darcy, a saucy piece of a waitress with a pretty smile and even prettier tits, came over to his table, pulling him from his thoughts as she plunked down another glass, took his money, and tossed him a wink. "What says' you and me have a bit o' fun tonight, Timmy, when I'm done 'ere?"

He knew he was in a sorry state when he shook his head rather than take her up on her offer. "Another time, love. I've things to sort out tonight. Here's a bit more for you to think kindly on me till then." He tossed a few extra notes onto her tray, returning her wink with one of his own.

"Ah, Timmy, you're a right one, you are. I may not hold your place, but I'll kick out the blighter warming me sheets when ye say the word."

"There's a lass."

He'd never been one to think so before, but Timmy was beginning to see the appeal of taking off to somewhere warm and peaceful, with nothing but a woman like Darcy and a supply of good ale to keep him company. Perhaps it was a sign of middle age. Too true he wasn't as young as he used to be. Sure, he could still scale the side of a building, and his fingers remained nimble enough when it counted. But how many more years did a man risk spitting in the face of fate before he set about to make a new life for himself?

Just then his instincts had him looking up toward the door. The man who'd come in was remarkable in his ordinariness and in his ability to blend in with any crowd. If Timmy hadn't been waiting for him, he couldn't have said if the chap had been there for hours or only now entered.

He put his attention back on his ale, and when the chair next to him was pulled out, he looked up into the eyes of his childhood friend.

"Can I stand you a pint, then, Freddy?"

"You can. Good to see you again, Timmy."

Timmy had only to look at Darcy to have the waitress come over, plunk a glass down in front of Freddy, take the money, and leave.

Lass knows how to keep mum, Timmy thought approvingly. He waited until she was well gone out of hearing then turned to Freddy.

"So, what do you have for me?"

"You'd think in these times of bleedin' fancy technology, what with everyone having a computer and printer of their own, that it'd be easier to leave off as one man and become another. It's not. What used to take weeks or months to follow up on is bloody instant now, and the loopholes we all used to count on being there have been sewn right shut, well enough. Mind, we can still do it. But it's a lot more involved and expensive than it used to be."

Timmy nodded slowly. He was still exploring his options and had decided to contact his old friend, who'd been out of the game for a bit, as opposed to going to someone more connected but less known to him.

"How expensive?" he asked now.

"More than ten, closer to twenty."

Twenty thousand pounds was a hell of a lot of money to pay for a new identity. He had more than that put by, of course. Timmy Sykes may never have gone to university, but he wasn't stupid. Besides, the put-by was only pounds and pence. On the other hand, an early funeral was too steep a price to pay for remaining the same man he'd been born.

"How long would it take?"

Freddy sat forward, his pose one of a friend confiding to a friend. "Could take about a month. I've a place in mind, tucked into a corner of nowhere in the Cotswolds, where you could wait. You'd be safe enough there. No one about but family, and they'd take a care."

"I'm not sure if it's what I'm going to do or not." He thought back to that last meeting in that fancy French hotel room. He knew that once word came of the Singer woman's death, he'd be on short time, no doubt about it. Aside from his belief that he'd be next on the list for that sadistic bastard, Irons, he'd be guilty as an accessory to murder at that point. Hell, the bloody cops could ratchet up the charge to conspiracy, and he'd be tried as if he was a buggering terrorist.

But then so, too, would Abbott—if the sense of things he got from the man was true.

"Just say the word, mate. It's been a bit, but I'm sure of my contacts and sure of the course. One word, and we'll get to it."

Timmy sat back. Before he made any final decision, he thought it might just be worth a bit of snooping about to see how Peter Abbott felt about all of this.

Turning to Freddy, Timmy raised his mug. "Here's to old friends. I'll let you know my decision, by and by."

Freddy raised his mug in turn. "Old friends, then. See that you watch your back, Timmy. I've no desire to wake you."

That, Timmy thought as he nodded, was definitely something worth drinking to.

Chapter 7

"I thought you asked me to meet you here so that we'd save time getting to the theatre."

"And you fell for that line?"

Pamela laughed softly as she stretched, her body feeling loose and limber and incredibly luxurious against the sheets.

She'd arrived at Dylan's penthouse just a half hour before, eager for another evening spent in his company. They were to eat dinner then head out to the Academy of Music and a live production of "Mama Mia." It shouldn't have surprised her that Dylan had swept her into a kiss and then into his bed. It seemed they couldn't be alone together anywhere and keep their hands—or their lips—off each other.

She turned her head slightly, a pleased smile taking over her face when she saw how utterly destroyed Dylan looked. "I did fall for that line. I hope you really *do* have those tickets, because I really want to see that show. I love the music of Abba."

"Got tickets. Not sure I have the energy to move, though."

Just as Pamela turned from her back to her side, Dylan flipped over and gathered her close. He pushed her onto her back again and loomed over her.

"You moved very well just then."

"I seem to have amazing energy whenever I think about having you under me."

In the last few days, Dylan hadn't given a single miscue, and Pamela had pretty much convinced herself that all the doubts and questions she'd had about him before really were the product of her own imagination, after all.

In the last week, they'd spent some of every day together, including more than a couple of nights snuggled up in Dylan's king-sized bed.

And every day, she fell just a little bit more under his spell.

"Traffic in this city being what it is, it's going to take us about fifteen minutes by cab to get there," Pamela said, trying to get them back on track. But then she gave in to temptation, and because he was so close, stretched up and licked the side of his neck. His response was instantaneous. He settled more fully on top of her, his erection cozying against the juncture of her thighs.

"I have a limo standing by. Rico, the driver, can make it in five." His words trailed off as he moved his hips and lowered his head.

"Oh good." Whatever else she'd been about to say was drowned in the flavor of him as his mouth took hers in a mind-numbing kiss.

* * * *

Dylan chuckled, feeling not at all embarrassed by the woman next to him dancing instead of walking as they exited the theatre into the warm summer night.

"You really do love the music of Abba," he said the moment she came up for air.

"I do. Wasn't that wonderful! I'd heard it was a great production, but it's even better than I thought it would be. And oh, wasn't it fantastic that *everyone* in the audience was singing along?"

Her exuberance tickled him. More and more he was finding it difficult to reconcile the woman laughingly looking up at him with the woman who had conned a half a million dollars from his brother before dumping him. He pushed the unpleasant thought away, choosing to ignore the fact that he was once more denying reality.

"That was a first for me," he said, picking up their conversation. "I never attended any rock concerts as a teen. Mother was very strict on that."

"Poor Dylan! Being surrounded by forty- and fifty-something fans singing their hearts out at the tops of their lungs for the last couple of hours." Her laughter and her smile were contagious.

"Well, your voice isn't that bad, and you did seem to know all the words."

Truth was, Dylan wasn't sure what he was most pleased about— that Pamela had enjoyed herself so much or that she'd not been able to hear him humming along with the music, too.

The night was clear and warm. Checking his watch, he saw that they were outside a bit earlier than he'd thought they'd be. The crowd was slow in leaving the theatre, heading to parking lots and waiting cabs. It was almost as if no one wanted to let the musical go. *No sense in calling for the car.* Rico was likely already on his way, and calling wouldn't bring him any faster. Looking kitty-corner across the street, Dylan spotted an older man selling flowers from a portable cart. Following impulse, he brought Pamela's hand to his lips and kissed it. "Wait here for a moment. I'll be right back." She looked past him to the vendor then gave him a shy smile and kissed his cheek.

"How sweet."

Traffic wasn't exceptionally heavy, even for a Friday evening in the middle of Philadelphia. The city held a wealth of theatres and restaurants, some of them new since he'd last worked in this city. When a space opened up, he sprinted across the street to the flower vendor.

Unlike similar peddlers he'd seen in various cities across Europe, this man seemed all business. "Flowers for your lady?"

The vendor nodded toward Pamela, proving he had a keen observational eye. "Absolutely. What's freshest?"

"They're all fresh, Mister. Picked them up from the wholesaler a couple of hours ago. What does the lady like?"

Dylan blinked. It was difficult to remember that he and Pamela had only days between them instead of months. He took a quick look over his shoulder. She wiggled her fingers in a wave back to him.

In the short time they'd been dating, the topic of flowers had never come up. Returning the eagle-eyed stare of the middle-aged vendor, he beat down his embarrassment. "We're pretty new to each other, and I have to confess I have no idea what kind of flowers she likes."

"Maybe you can figure out what kind of flower is like her, then. You have your rose types—ultra feminine with expensive tastes; you've got your orchid types—elegant and a bit untouchable; and you've got your lily types—fresh, adventurous with a touch of innocence."

Philosophy from a street vendor. Dylan turned his attention to Pamela again and couldn't help but smile. She was still swaying to the music that had filled the opera house so recently. He knew it was foolish on his part, given the reason *for* his courtship of her, but based on the thumbnail sketches just presented by the flower seller, he'd have to say that Pamela was almost pure lily.

"Lilies, please." The bouquet of white glistening flowers carried a subtle scent that put him in mind of springtime and lush green meadows. As the vendor was wrapping paper around the dripping stems, Dylan looked over his shoulder to smile at Pamela one more time.

The sound of an engine revving raced a shiver down his spine. Lights flashed bright and bold a block down Locust Street. As he watched, a late-model dark sedan peeled away from its curbside parking spot, the driver accelerating recklessly. Just before the intersection with Broadway, the car swerved hard right, heading straight for Pamela.

There was no time to warn her. Screams and the shouts of onlookers filled the air. In crystal clarity, Dylan watched as the dark car bore down on her.

Pamela moved with seconds to spare, catapulting herself out of the way, and in one smooth motion came down on the pavement on her side and rolled closer to the building. The car swerved left, squealed its brakes, and sped off down the street.

Dylan had never run so fast in all his life.

Pushing through the small crowd that had quickly surrounded Pamela, he dropped to his knees and pulled her into his arms.

"I'm all right. I'm all right. God, that was close."

"Damned drunken teenagers!" a man in the group spat. A chorus of agreements echoed through the throng like a wave.

"Are you hurt?" Dylan didn't care if everyone saw his hands shaking. He pulled back so he could see her face when he asked, "Do you need the hospital?"

"No, Dylan, I'm okay. Really. He didn't touch me. I'm just shaky, and I'll likely have a bruise on my hip. But I'm fine."

He helped her to her feet. Watching carefully, he held onto her until he knew she could stand on her own. She seemed more embarrassed than anything and unused to being fussed over by so many people. Someone handed her the purse she'd dropped when she'd made her miraculous leap.

"Anyone see a license plate?"

Dylan turned at the voice of the flower-seller. To Dylan he said, "You forgot your flowers," as he handed the bundle to him.

"That asshole was going too fast for me to catch a plate number," one older man said.

"There wasn't one, at least not on the back of the car," his female companion observed.

"That's against the law. Out-of-state bastard!" This last was nearly spat by an older man who needed a cane to help him walk. "Kid should be horsewhipped. Drunken bum. That's what's wrong with kids today. Too much money, too much booze, and not enough discipline." Another chorus of agreeing sounds accompanied this pronouncement.

"You're sure you're all right?" Dylan asked Pamela again.

"I'm fine." She turned and offered a smile to all the good Samaritans who'd gathered around her. "Thank you all for coming to my aid."

The spectators began to disperse, some continuing to discuss the incident as they walked.

Dylan sighed in relief when, moments later, the hotel's limo pulled up.

"Are those for me?"

Dylan looked at the flowers in his hand as if he'd never seen them before. Shaking his head, he said, "Yeah." Letting out a deep breath, he handed them to her. "Let's get back to the hotel. There's a doctor on call. I think I'll invite him up to our suite. I want to be sure you're all right."

"Hey."

Something of his tension must have gotten through to her, for she stroked his face and then kissed him. "He missed me, Dylan. I just hope he doesn't hit some other poor, innocent bystander on his way home to sleep it off."

Dylan looked into her eyes for a long moment. "Yeah, me too," he said at last.

Once in the backseat of the limo, Dylan pulled her close, wrapping a protective arm around her. He could see no reason to disabuse Pamela of her belief that what had just happened to her was the result of some kid who'd had too much to drink. There was no doubt in his mind that she did really believe just that.

But he'd been across the street, had watched the entire scenario play out in perfect clarity. And he knew for certain that what had nearly happened had been no accident. The short glimpse he'd gotten of the driver of that late-model Buick showed him a man who appeared middle aged and had been sporting a beard.

The man had deliberately aimed his car directly for Pamela.

For the first time since meeting her, it occurred to Dylan that his brother wasn't the only man Pamela had taken for a ride in her career as *The Seductress*. Now he had to wonder which one had decided to strike out for his own vengeance.

* * * *

Pamela relished the sensation of hot water cascading over her skin. Nearly one a.m., she could have left this ritual until later in the morning, except that she was beginning to feel her muscles tighten up from her tumble to the pavement.

The doctor Dylan had summoned had given her a clean bill of health. She was practically unscathed. She'd been right about the bruise on her left hip, as one had already begun to form. The only other damage she'd suffered was a scrape on her left knee. Doctor Westerly had treated that with antibiotic ointment and left not very long after he'd arrived.

Pamela promptly poured Dylan a full glass of brandy and excused herself to shower. She wasn't going to tell him she was beginning to hurt. She'd spotted a bottle of aspirin on the shelf earlier. She'd just pop a couple of the pills before rejoining him.

She thought it was entirely possible that near miss had scared Dylan more than it had her.

She couldn't keep the smile off her face as she thought of the way he'd been practically coddling her since the incident. It felt good to be the object of his complete and total attention. She'd never felt as important to anyone—no, to any *man*—in her life.

Sound alerted her. Then strong male hands slid around from behind and cupped her breasts. Sighing, she leaned back against a firm, naked chest, the water and the man working together to intoxicate her completely.

"I thought I'd conduct my own examination," Dylan whispered in her ear. One hand left her only long enough to grab hold of the soap.

Rather than smoothing it across her breasts, he brought the bar to the curls covering her mound and began a slow, gentle massage.

"Oh, God." She felt the strength leave her legs and had no choice but to lean against him. Reaching up and behind, her arms encircled his neck.

"Open for me."

His roughly whispered command heated her blood, and she could no more refuse him than she could stop breathing. His long and agile fingers explored and delved while he used the fragrant bar to smooth and rub.

Crying out, she came, the orgasm sudden and sharp, shooting sparks along her nerve endings and tingling her toes.

"You're so hot for me, baby. Do you have any idea how much it turns me on to be able to shoot you up and over so quickly?"

"Dylan!" He kept his hand busy on her at the same time his tongue began to play along the shell of her ear. "Oh, God, I can't!"

His chuckle was pure primal male as he wrapped his arm around her and worked two fingers into her.

"Oh, I think you can. I think you can come for me again and again."

Just as she was about to dispute that, arousal ignited anew, this time like heavy, molten syrup that slowly spread over and around and through, until it filled every inch of her. Moving her hips against his hand, she tightened her grip around his neck, tiny mews of need working up from her throat in perfect cadence with each fresh abrasion to her woman-flesh.

"Do you want me, Pamela?"

"Yes. Yes, I want you."

It no longer mattered to her that her body felt bruised and sore from her earlier mishap. The only thing that mattered was that she feel Dylan inside her. He rinsed her and then dried them both haphazardly. Did he know she could barely stand, let alone walk? He must, for he carried her through the door of the bathroom those few feet to the bed.

When he laid her on her back, when he loomed over her, she could give him only animalistic sounds of want and need. He took nearly no time at all to roll on the condom.

When he splayed her legs wide and looked down at her, she shivered, a sense of vulnerability entwining around the heat.

"Say my name. Tell me you want me, and say my name."

Through the layers of seduction and sensuality, the hint that he felt vulnerable, too, caught her unawares.

"Say my name, Pamela."

There was desperation in him which she didn't understand. She didn't need to. It was little enough, this demand, little enough for all he'd given her, all he was coming to mean to her.

"Dylan. I need you inside me, Dylan."

"Only me?"

"Yes. Yes, only you. *Please*!"

He slid into her, body and soul. Pamela wrapped herself around him and rode his thrusts as her climax unravelled her completely.

Chapter 8

"I think you're the first man I've ever met who actually likes to shop."

Pamela's comment only pricked Dylan's conscience a little. He wasn't really overly fond of shopping. But he couldn't very well tell her that. Since the attempt on her life the other night—and he had no doubt whatsoever it had been a *deliberate* attempt on her life—he was loath to let her go anywhere without him.

But she had, of course, and Dylan had suffered a hundred years worth of anguish in the last few days, every time she was out of his sight. This morning, before picking her up at her sister's apartment, he'd taken steps to have her followed. He'd used the same agency he'd employed to help him locate her in the first place, and if his motives had somehow changed since then, he shuffled that bit of thinking off into a corner marked "irrelevant."

It wasn't, of course. He'd begun to suspect that, since the incident outside the Academy of Music, his entire focus—where Pamela Singer was concerned—had shifted.

Compared with what had nearly happened to her, his vengeance seemed insignificant. Yes, he wanted things made right for Dmitri; he wanted his brother vindicated and Pamela somehow brought to account for what she'd done to him. But not at the cost of her life.

He gazed up a couple of blocks and across the street at the park-like setting of Rittenhouse Square. The midsummer day was sunny and warm, and the park teemed with people. Some were native Philadelphians, enjoying the open air as they walked dogs, read, or lounged about, listening to music or just sprawled out, catching some rest. Some were tourists, the lifeblood of many businesses, including his own.

"Let's go in here."

Pamela took his hand and dragged him into another shop. He'd been in enough high-end boutiques with his mother and various other women to recognize the labels. Chloe, Gaultier, Yamamoto, Dries Van Noten, Stella McCartney. It wasn't only in the discipline of art that his mother had tried to educate him.

The store, Joan Shepp, was neat and spacious and busy.

"What is it you're looking for?" he asked, noting the way Pamela's gaze seemed to sweep the entire area, as if she was trying to decide where to start.

"Oh, I'm not going to buy anything. I just love to look."

Something in her tone intrigued him. "You just look?"

"Mostly, yes. I love to see what the designers are coming up with, not just in clothes, but shoes and purses, jewelry and whatever. But I buy only if something *really* grabs me. "

He'd been around enough women who seemed to live by the motto: "She who has the most stuff wins," that Pamela's offhand attitude didn't make sense to him. He would have sworn, with everything he'd come to believe about her, that she'd be a staunch supporter of the Acquisition Creed.

"If you're not going to buy anything, why are we here?"

"Dylan, you don't have to go through life *accumulating* things. Sometimes it's more fun just to look and imagine." She pulled out a jacket and held it up against herself. She pivoted around to catch her reflection in the mirror.

If she'd asked him, he'd have told her the truth. The jacket would look stunning on her. But she didn't ask, instead just letting herself gaze at it in the mirror, an almost winsome smile on her face, before putting it back and seeking out the next item.

Unsure what game Pamela was playing, he let his eyes linger for a moment on the jacket. Catching sight of the price tag, he didn't think eight hundred and fifty dollars was all that much, considering the label. Then he thought he understood what this exercise was all about. He didn't mind. It wouldn't, after all, be the first time for him.

So he said what he believed was his line. "Let me buy this for you."

"Oh, absolutely not! Are you out of your mind? It's eight hundred and fifty dollars!"

This last she'd said in a whisper, her look so horrified he had to smile. "I can afford it, Pamela."

"Well, so can I, but that's not the point."

She walked over to a rack of dresses, sorting through it, holding one shimmery bit of red nothing up. "Now this would look wonderful on Alba. Of course, I'd never be able to get her to wear it."

"Why not?"

"Because it shows a good amount of cleavage and leg, and Alba's very shy. An unexpected trait, given her background and her profession, some would say. Maybe someday we'll get her to let loose a little."

"Now I'll have to ask you about her background and her profession, because you've got my curiosity roused."

"Do I? Maybe I'll tell you, then. When we know each other better."

Leaving the dresses, she made her way over to a display counter that showcased accessories, some of them colorful and sparkly—two things he would have sworn women found irresistible.

Watching the way she was looking at the pieces within the showcase, the truth began to dawn. "You're really not going to let me buy anything for you, are you?"

"That's not true." She gave him a bright smile and a kiss on the cheek. "I'll let you buy me lunch."

"Lunch."

She tilted her head to the side. "Yes. Just lunch"—She checked her watch—"in about an hour. But there are a couple more stores I want to visit first. Come on."

Dylan followed in her wake as she left the store. Her subtle scent carried back to him on the breeze, and he had to work hard to keep his arousal under control. More and more she confused him. Shaking his head, he let her lead him where she would—literally and for now, at any rate.

* * * *

Billy O'Reilly lounged against the large maple, headphones in his ears, his head bouncing as if in time with the music from his boom box. Sunglasses pushed tight against his face, and a lean, fair-haired build all worked to his advantage. Anyone looking at him wouldn't really notice him at all.

He wished he had more time to take in this so-called City of Brotherly Love. He'd been to New York and had ventured into Boston in the last couple of years. But this was his first visit to Philadelphia.

At least he'd had the chance to take in the Liberty Bell.

He liked what he could see of this neighbourhood. These were the kind of shops, if he played his cards right and was enterprising enough, that he'd be able to patronize on a regular basis soon. From what he had seen so far, the stores of Rittenhouse Row sold nothing but the best.

Billy O'Reilly believed he deserved the best.

He'd been doing contract work for the last three years. Finally, with *this* contract, he was moving up into the circle of clientele that paid top dollar.

One hit here, followed by one in Greece. Then nothing would stand in the way of the good life for Mrs. O'Reilly's little boy.

His gaze left the storefront long enough to follow the progress of a dark blue Buick as it secured a parking spot between Seventeenth and Eighteenth. He nodded slightly then ran a hand through his hair. *Just a few more minutes, mate.*

He'd been following the woman all morning, and he was pretty certain he had her rhythm down. His steps casual, he strolled from the tree to the path and then slowly made his way to the sidewalk. He knew he looked like an ordinary bloke who had nothing but time.

He strolled east, toward the river, just as the woman came out of the store up ahead and on the opposite side of the street.

O'Reilly smiled when she and her companion came toward him, their pace casual. They crossed Seventeenth Street, and his eyes never left them. He'd nearly reached the car but kept them in his peripheral for a moment. Then he stopped and looked behind him, as if he'd forgotten something. The woman and the man crossed Eighteenth and immediately veered toward the entrance of the corner shop, climbing the stairs and entering it.

Timing would be key. He just hoped Asher did his part. The man sure as hell hadn't timed it well the other night. He'd missed Ms. Singer by mere *seconds.*

So far, the woman was acting as if her near miss had been some sort of accident—a matter of being in the wrong place at the wrong time. After today, she'd be dead, and the cops might just put two and two together, so O'Reilly had made contingency plans. He knew exactly where he'd do it—just around the corner on Eighteenth. Two shots to the head, which would take less than four seconds to deliver. Thirty seconds post-hit, they'd be on John F. Kennedy Boulevard heading west. Two minutes after that, tops, they'd be on the expressway. It would take them a couple of hours to reach their secondary base. There, they'd wipe down the Buick before setting the timer for the explosion. Tonight he'd be in New York City, and tomorrow he'd be back in London.

Planning and timing, O'Reilly thought now. It was all just a matter of planning and timing.

They were still inside the shop, so he turned and headed to the car. Opening the door, O'Reilly got in, tossing his radio into the backseat.

"They're in there," Billow said, pointing.

He'd kept the car running, so that was something. "I'm thinking that she'll head down to Eighteenth. Everything east of here on Walnut looks to be under construction."

"As soon as they do, I'll move. Traffic isn't particularly heavy today. I think this will be a snap."

"So do I." O'Reilly lowered his window and pulled the Glock out of his holster.

* * * *

"Do you have any idea where we're going?"

Pamela flashed a smile at Dylan. He'd been very patient with her today. In the mood to window-shop and cruise some of the more exclusive venues, he'd been a real trooper going along with her as he had. Even when she'd teased him earlier about liking to shop, he'd reacted manly, saying nothing to disabuse her of her silly notion.

They were standing on the sidewalk, having just come out of Anthropologie, waiting for the light to change.

"Of course I know where we're going. It's this great shop called Leehe Fai. They have everything, very chic, *and* they're 'boyfriend' friendly. They have chairs and magazines. So all you testosterone-makers can commiserate and make male-bonding noises over pictures of cars and wrestling men and whatever else those publications offer. "

"Boyfriend? Is that what I am? Your *boy*friend?"

He'd put emphasis on the word "boy." Pamela laughed. "I'd say you're doing a reasonable impression of one. There it is. You can see it from here. Just a block and half to go, and we'll be there."

"Tria is just a bit farther, if memory serves. How about, after you finish your shopping without buying anything, we go there? They've got the best selection of cheese, good wine, and even some excellent beer. Or if you're in the mood for more substantial fare, we could go back to Rouge. It's on the other side of Walnut, right across from the park, and has al fresco dining. Their burger is fantastic."

The light changed, and they crossed the street and then turned north. "Decisions, decisions. I think I'm in the mood for a good burger. And maybe a cab back to your place after?"

"You've got a deal."

Just the thought of going back to Dylan's place had her juices flowing. Following an impulse, she swung back in the midst of her next step forward and stretched up to kiss him.

The loud crack and the burst of stone close to her face made her jump. The next instant, Dylan pulled her to the ground as another crack exploded.

* * * *

His heart slammed into his chest. When the tires squealed, he dared to look up. A dark blue car was careening around a corner up ahead, and in less than a second, sped out of sight. Screams and running feet still echoed up and down the block. Dylan didn't care about any of that. He had only one concern at the moment, and that was the quivering, shivering woman under him.

He lifted up, looked down, and saw blood.

"Pamela!"

"I'm all right. I'm all right. My ears are ringing, though."

Her words had tumbled out, directed to the ground as she tried to get up on all fours, presumably to stand.

"You're not all right. You're bleeding."

The coldness flooding through him was a welcome sensation. It locked his emotions in a cage allowing him clear, concise thought.

Pamela managed to turn over and sit up on her own. A stream of blood trickled down the left side of her face. Sitting on his haunches, Dylan pulled out his handkerchief. Gently cupping her chin in his hand, he lifted her head and turned it slightly. As he dabbed at the wound, some of his fear left. She had a nick in her hair line, not terribly deep, but head wounds inevitably bled profusely.

"Does it hurt?"

"No, not really. Just a bit of a sting is all."

It didn't surprise him that she'd begun to shake.

"I've called the police," a woman said as she knelt beside them. She had a shawl in her hands and placed it around Pamela's shoulders. "Tiffany is bringing out my first aid kit—ah, here it is."

"Second time this month," the woman Dylan assumed was Tiffany said. "When are the damned cops going to do something about these bastards? Shooting up the city left, right, and center. This keeps up, there'll be no customers for any of us, at all."

Dylan heard sirens in the distance. He removed his handkerchief from Pamela's head and shifted over slightly.

"I'm Iris, by the way," the woman said as she used a gauze pad soaked in alcohol to dab at the cut on Pamela's head.

"Was anybody else hurt?"

Pamela's question came out as a shaky whisper.

"Nope, you're the only casualty," Iris informed her cheerfully.

"There was no one else near us." Dylan couldn't keep the edge out of his voice. Now that he knew Pamela wasn't seriously hurt, his anger kicked in. He remained silent while Iris put a light bandage on the cut. Once the Good Samaritan got to her feet and was out of hearing range, he said, "You'll talk to the police."

Confusion swam in Pamela's eyes when she looked up at him. "Yes. Of course I will. But I didn't see what happened."

The screech of tires announced the arrival of the first responders. The cops began to clear the spectators that had gathered around them. Dylan knew they had only a few seconds left to be alone. Wanting to make sure she understood him, he lifted her chin again, so that she could see he was serious.

"I'm sure you didn't. But you have to have some idea who's trying to kill you."

Chapter 9

"Why didn't you report the incident the other night?"

Officer Markel wore a no-nonsense expression that perfectly matched his spit-and-polish blue uniform. He was waiting, pen poised over his pad, as if the words Pamela was about to utter were going to be the most memorable in history.

"I thought it was just a drunk driver. Everybody outside the theatre did. Then the car was gone so fast, and no one got a license plate number. I didn't think to call the police to report that something *almost* happened."

"If you'd reported the incident, dispatch could have issued a bolo. A 'be on the lookout,'" he explained when she frowned up at him.

"But if he was still driving erratically, wouldn't your officers have tried to pull him over, regardless of a report having been filed?"

It was clear that Officer Markel wasn't impressed by her logic. Pamela had a headache, she was tired, and she just wanted to go someplace where she could sulk and feel sorry for herself for five *damn* minutes.

"Well." Markel closed his note-book and looked from her—he'd been kind enough, at least, to open the back door of his cruiser and allow her to sit—to Dylan, who was standing by the trunk of the cop car, arms folded, an unhappy expression on his face. "My cop instincts tell me that these two incidents *might* be related. But we can't know for certain, as in neither case is there a clear description of the vehicle. Also, it pains me to admit there have been several incidents in this area in the last few months that we consider to be gang-related. The shots fired *toward* you could have been another such incident and may have just been a case of you being in the wrong place at the wrong time."

"There wasn't anybody else in the line of fire *but* us."

Dylan had said that twice now—three times if she counted before the police arrived. With each repetition, he sounded angrier than the time before. He'd been in a bad mood since just before the cops arrived. Of course, she really couldn't blame him. Being shot at wasn't conducive to good humor.

But you have to have some idea who's trying to kill you.

Dylan's words came back to her, and she couldn't for the life of her figure out what he'd meant by them. Maybe they were said in the stress of the moment. Because Pamela had no idea who could want her dead, which was what she'd said to Officer Markel, when to placate Dylan, he'd half-heartedly asked her just that a few minutes ago.

Her attention was yanked back to the present. If the scowl on his face was any measure, Officer Markel didn't seem to like Dylan's anger any better than he'd liked her logic.

"So you've said, Mr. Pierce." The officer took a moment to open his note-pad again, flip through some pages. "You said that there was no one between the two of you and the store, Leehe Fai." He closed the notebook and gave Dylan a level stare. "However, you can't say with any certainty whether or not there were people behind you on the sidewalk when the shots were fired."

"Can we go?" Pamela had had enough. Her head was pounding, her entire body was crying out for a hot bath, and she sure as hell wasn't interested in a pissing contest between Dylan and this cop right now.

Office Markel shifted his stance, giving Pamela room so she could stand up and get away from the cruiser. "Stay available for further questioning, and let us know if you leave town."

Pamela nodded. Not sure where she was going to go next, she just wanted to be gone from *there*. Dylan solved the dilemma for her by taking her arm and leading her down the block. After only a couple of steps, she saw the hotel's white limo. The driver hurried around to open the back door for them.

"Can I give you a rain check on lunch?" She really didn't feel like eating anything right now. All she wanted was some aspirin and a dark room to sleep in.

"Rico, take us over to the emergency room at Jefferson University Hospital."

Pamela turned her head at the imperious tone, only to encounter Dylan's implacable expression. He was holding his cell phone to his ear.

"I don't need the emergency room. I need aspirin and sleep. Besides, those places keep you waiting all day."

Again, he didn't answer her immediately but spoke into the phone. "Ted? Dylan. We're on our way now." He snapped the phone closed and eyed her critically. "You've just suffered a head wound, so you get the emergency room. Don't worry, though, we won't be waiting at all. A doctor's going to meet us. My family has connections."

"Oh goody." The lack of tenderness in his eyes irritated her.

"So first you get your head examined. And then, lady, you and I are going to talk."

* * * *

Dylan had so many emotions churning through him it was a wonder he didn't explode. The icy demeanor that had come with those gunshots was finally cracking, giving way to a mixture of anger and relief.

He was able to hang on to his temper as he opened the door to his hotel suite and motioned for Pamela to enter ahead of him.

He thought he was doing a pretty good job of keeping his spleen from venting. The door slipped from his grip, and the resulting slam echoed in the quiet of the penthouse. *Okay, that was probably a clue to my mood.*

"Look, I'm not too happy about being shot at, either," Pamela spat, and oh, was he glad that she'd taken the gloves off first. "But you don't see *me* throwing a temper tantrum all over the damn place."

He rounded on her and let her see exactly how pissed he was. "I told you to talk to the police!"

"I did talk to the police. You were right there!"

"Enough! In a few minutes I'm going to call a friend of mine who's a detective on the Philadelphia police force. But first, we're going to lay out just exactly what it is you're going to tell him." Noting the total confusion on Pamela's face, he wanted to shake her. He'd given her enough of a clue so she'd understand what he meant. He was tired of this pretense she seemed to be living. He was tired of being scared out of his wits.

"I don't know what the hell you're talking about. Between the two of us, you're more likely to have a target painted on your back than I am. As you said, your family has *connections.*"

Her tone suggested she knew all about his family—which she must, he reasoned. How could she not? According to Dmitri, she'd been practically living with his brother. *Now we're getting somewhere.*

"Yes, I imagine from where you're sitting it looks that way. But I'm not the one who's built a reputation by wheedling money out of older men. They sure as hell don't call *me The Seductress.* You had to know that at some point it was all going to catch up with you. I thought I'd be the one to call you to account. That was my plan. After what you did to my brother, I came after you with vengeance on my mind. But I've found, over the last few weeks, I've come to care for you more than I counted on and more than I probably should have. Score another one for *The Seductress.* But even knowing everything about you, I don't want to see you hurt, and I sure as *hell* don't want to see you killed. So when I call Michael, you're to tell him the name of every man you've conned, so he can get working on finding out which one—either the man himself or his relatives—is trying to kill you."

She was a hell of a good actress, he'd give her that. How she managed to make her complexion turn that pasty white, he didn't know.

"Your brother? You planned…you think I…" She stopped talking, and instead, slowly sank into a chair. Her eyes focused on the floor. He imagined it was a shock for her to be faced with his knowledge of her. He was sorry for that, but the game had turned deadly serious.

"Now, we can pretty well figure that Dmitri isn't behind these attacks. I'd be the first one to admit he has a temper, but he'd never do anything to hurt or harm a woman. I'd stake my life on that. So—"

"Dmitri Andropolis is your brother."

Something in the lifeless quality of her voice bothered him. But he'd started down this road, and the sooner she understood that he knew everything about her, the better. Then they could move on to keeping her alive.

"He is. We'll discuss the half a million dollars you relieved him of later. But for right now—"

"No."

For the second time, Pamela interrupted him. Only this time there was nothing lifeless about her. As she got to her feet, her eyes blazed in anger.

"You think you have it all figured out. You think you have *me* figured out. But you don't know jack shit."

"Pamela, drop the self-righteous indignation act, okay? Maybe I understand, a little. You grew up in the system, bouncing from one foster home to the next until you were eleven. I can understand how never having anything can drive a person to want to acquire things. And technically, there's nothing illegal in what you've done. Why shouldn't you profit from giving older men what they want—"

She was on him in a flash, the crack of her slap exploding in the room. She'd taken him completely unawares, and his cheek stung madly.

"So I'm a con artist and a whore, and you *came after me* for vengeance. For your brother. For Dmitri Andropolis. Because you think *I* wronged *him* somehow?"

Dylan nearly drowned in the sudden urge to defend himself. Before he could draw his next breath, she stepped back, both hands covering her mouth.

"It wasn't real," she said after a moment. "*None* of it was real. You were…playing a role? The entire time. I let you inside my body, and you were just playing a *game*?"

How had he lost control of the situation? And why did each word she hurled leave him feeling more and more slimy?

"You bastard. What you did was even worse than what he did."

He didn't expect her to try to leave. He'd thought that once they'd cleared the air she'd cooperate. Her *life* was at stake; she had to understand that.

Dylan caught her just before she opened the door. When she cringed, when she threw up her hands as if to ward off a blow, he grabbed her other arm and pulled her around to face him.

"You think I'm going to *hit* you?" He knew true horror laced his words. He'd never raised a hand to a woman in his life.

"Yesterday, I would have sworn not. But today, I don't know. I don't know you. You're a stranger to me. A stranger who already has his hands on me. *Let go.*"

Dylan felt as if he'd been slammed in the gut. Tears filled her eyes, and the look she sent him made him take a half step back.

"We're done here."

"We're not." He placed one hand on the door to prevent her from leaving. "Someone is trying to kill you. Let me call my friend. Let me help you."

"Take your hand off the door."

There was finality in her tone. Perhaps it would be good to give her a few hours to cool off. Slowly, he lowered his hand and took a step back.

Turning just before she left, she shot him a look that was more pain than anger, a look that made him want to gather her close and make all the hurt go away.

"Go to hell, Dylan Pierce. I never want to see you again."

For a long moment, he stood frozen to the spot. *She didn't really mean that. It was likely just her temper talking.*

But Dylan had the sinking sensation that he'd somehow just made a very serious mistake.

* * * *

It was buried on the inside of the *Philadelphia Daily Times*.

O'Reilly had taken a stroll from the hotel in Queens, in need of cigarettes and information. He'd tuned in to the news networks offered on the hotel's cable television service, but the story hadn't been carried on any of the national networks.

As he opened the paper, the knuckles of his right hand protested. They were still red and raw. Asher's face had been a mite harder than anticipated. But in the end, the other man had lost the fight, and consciousness, and then—O'Reilly smiled—his life.

Bloody wanker should never have missed the bitch with his car. Billy thought it likely a wise thing to have done away with the man. Now, when he reported back, his client would see his attention to detail. No loose ends left. Satisfaction guaranteed.

Bringing his focus back to the article, he sat forward slowly as he read the short news article. "*Police confirm there was an incident yesterday around the noon hour in the busy and popular Rittenhouse Row area of the center city, with shots being fired from a passing vehicle. No fatalities were reported, but one woman did receive superficial injuries in the attack. The mayor, at a press conference held later in the afternoon, has vowed that he will not rest until gang violence in the city is brought under control."*

Fuck. O'Reilly crumpled the paper and flung it on the floor. *Superficial injuries*? Son of a bitch! Heart pounding, he began to pace the room. *Fuck, fuck, fuck.* He'd been certain he'd hit her. He'd gotten off two quick shots, and she'd gone down with the first!

No, it was cool. He could blow off this failure. He could tell his client Asher had fucked up, and he'd judged it more efficient to deal with the man immediately. Likely Ms. Singer would be returning to France soon, and it was in France where she'd meet her end at the hands of Billy O'Reilly. Better over there, really. He knew the territory—France or England; he was equally at home in either country. Pursuing the target to Philadelphia had been a whim, anyway, a bid on Billy's part to show himself as an international player. Yes, that would work. *Blame Asher.* He nearly laughed aloud as he remembered that cheesy line from an old movie: Dead men tell no tales. Asher was dead as a crispy critter could be, and he sure as hell would tell no more tales.

Reaching up, Billy wiped the sweat from his forehead. He forced himself to breathe deeply, until the fine trembling that had taken over his body calmed.

It was nearly eleven at night. He had to be at the airport by three a.m. Too wired to sleep, Billy decided he might as well get an early start. He'd not unpacked his single suitcase. Leaving was just a matter of scooping up the battered bag and catching a cab.

Everything was going to be all right. He was still in control. Sooner or later, Ms. Singer was going to go home.

And Billy O'Reilly would be waiting for her.

Chapter 10

"Hunter, my brother's secretary just informed me he's on vacation."

"Yes, I believe he is. As a vice-president of the company, he's pretty much free to come and go as he pleases."

Dmitri Andropolis caught the subtle edge in Hunter Symington's voice. In the last little while, he'd had cause to doubt the sincerity of the man he'd always considered a friend. His manner now was just the latest indication that all was not as it used to be.

"Be that as it may, my problem is the little bitch wouldn't tell me where he is or give me a number where he can be reached." As he held the receiver to his ear, Dmitri fought against the tide of seething anger that swirled within him.

Not that he didn't have cause for anger; of course, he did. But the time to give vent to his emotions, the time to seek blood for blood, was not now.

He'd bought himself some time, thanks to a lie. No one would touch him again as long as they believed that bitch Pamela had all their names. He didn't feel guilty, either, because this trouble was really all her fault anyway. If she'd known her place, if she'd behaved as a proper woman, then the plan he'd worked so hard to implement would even now have begun to pay off. When she'd ended their affair so unexpectedly, she'd ruined everything. That bastard Irons had paid him a visit, and he'd had to come up with a half a million dollars to placate his partners. He'd taken it from the company, of course. It had been a long time since he'd had that kind of money in his personal account.

The Moerae Corporation was *his* company. *His* birthright. Justin Pierce, his bastard of a stepfather, had fired him. Fired him for taking what was his *by right*. His grandfather Leandros—his mother's father—had begun what was now the Moerae Corporation with his hard work and his investment. When his mother had married Justin Pierce, she turned her life over to the man completely. Oh, he'd known from the first moment he'd met his new stepfather that here was an enemy to watch. And he'd been proven right last year when his grandfather had retired and handed everything over to Pierce instead of to him. He was a Leandros, while Pierce was an outsider and a foreigner.

Dmitri had never liked or trusted his mother's husband, but he'd done his best over the years to curry the man's favor by befriending his little bastard of a half brother. Perhaps it hadn't gained him as many points with the senior Pierce as he'd wanted, but he knew Dylan was devoted to him.

His brother had visited a few weeks ago, and Dmitri knew by the look in his eyes when he left, that something would soon be done. Maria Andropolis Pierce was deaf and dumb when it came to her firstborn son—but not when it came to the baby of the family.

Dmitri had waited long enough without hearing anything. That was why he was trying to get hold of Dylan now. It was past time for him to be reinstated into the company. He had expenses that needed to be met. Once he was back in his office, once he had access, he'd be able to infuse his personal account.

And the little bastard was on vacation? The sound of Hunter's voice pulled his attention back to the phone call.

"No, Justin ordered her not to divulge his son's whereabouts— especially to you. It seems he's worried you'll drag his beloved son into the middle of your latest fuck up. Frankly, I can't say that I blame him."

There was no imagining the animosity in Symington's voice this time. "You need to be a bit more careful of the way you speak to me, my friend. You forget your place. Now, tell me, Hunter. Where is Dylan?"

"I really have no idea exactly where he is, Dmitri. Perhaps you should try calling his cell phone. I know he'd be pleased to hear from you. Now if you'll excuse me, I have more important things to do than pay homage to your ego."

Incredulous, he listened to the sound of the dial tone for a few moments before he slammed down the receiver. Dmitri swore, trying to ignore the shaking of his hands and the quaking of his heart. If Hunter had turned against him too—

Pulling his cell phone out of his pocket, he thumbed through the numbers stored there. Realizing he didn't even have Dylan's, he threw the useless device across the room. He recalled that, not long ago, Dylan had given him the number, and he'd made a show of recording it. Of course, he'd thrown it out. Who would have thought the time would ever come when he'd actually *want* to call the little prick?

He'd been counting on his half brother to smooth things over with the family, and how lowering was that? He'd have to think of a way to get that number. In the meantime, he had a larger problem.

Dmitri was running depressingly low on cash. He walked over to his apartment's bar, poured himself a glass of scotch.

It was time, he thought, to take matters into his own hands. And he knew just where to start.

* * * *

The painting, from the baroque period, depicted a lively scene of celebration and near-debauchery. Created by one of the lesser-known Flemish painters in the first decade of the seventeenth century, this was by no means the largest or the most complex assignment Pamela had ever undertaken. The small private gallery just outside of Toulouse couldn't afford to pay her as much as she normally charged.

But the staff there had a true love of art. The gallery's owner, a widow with one of the most acerbic personalities Pamela had ever encountered, made up for her less-than-stellar people skills by being completely committed to keeping her small gallery open. No one would blame her if she decided to sell the pieces, and the building, and retire into better circumstances than she'd ever known. Instead, the woman kept her small oasis of art open to the public for a nominal charge as a memorial to her late husband.

This proved, Pamela supposed, that not *all* men were pricks.

She sat back on her haunches and rubbed her face with both hands.

In the week she'd been back from the States, she'd tried very hard to keep thoughts of *men* off her mind. She especially didn't want to think of a certain T, D, and H hotelier or his sexy body.

Why couldn't she succeed in that quest?

She'd left Dylan's penthouse last week and the country the next day. She'd held herself together until she'd unlocked her own front door. Then she'd thrown herself onto her bed and cried like a baby.

When she realized that four days had gone by and, not only had she *not* gone out to get groceries, but she'd not bothered to shower, either, she'd given herself a firm lecture.

No man was worth this much upset.

Dylan was.

Shaking her head, she told that inner voice to shut the hell up and turned her attention back to the art. Life was better when men were ignored. That was turning into a sad but true reality for her. Two men in a row now she'd misjudged.

In her personal opinion, three strikes and you're out was far too generous a standard. She thought two strikes were more than sufficient.

Taking up her digital camera, she centered the shot she needed, making sure she had the entire painting in view. When she was

The frigging bitch. Billy O'Reilly pushed himself deeper into the shadows, alone in the dark of night with his anger and his switchblade. It didn't matter how long he had to wait. It didn't matter that this was a kill he wouldn't be paid for.

This one was free. Pamela Singer had cost him his first shot at a place in the upper strata of contractors, and she was going to pay for that.

He'd been summoned to the office of The Provider and informed the client had secured another contractor. Then, as he'd been leaving, he'd been jumped by a man who'd beat bloody hell out of him. His attacker had left him with the taunt, "Let a bloody skirt get the best of you," whispered in an American accent. It had taken a few days for the swelling to go down enough that he could move about.

He owed Ms. Singer for that, too, so he'd play with her a bit before he offed her. She deserved to feel a little pain in return for the pain and inconvenience she'd caused him.

And maybe, if he was creative enough, he'd get other offers that would lead him where he knew he belonged.

If a man was crafty enough, he could carve out a slice of heaven for himself. *Carve out.* The words tickled him as he opened then closed his knife. Yes, he'd do some carving. *Just as soon as that bitch showed her face.*

Billy knew his mother's oft-cited "patience is a virtue" was true when, just a few moments later, his target emerged from her flat.

He'd been keeping watch for a couple of days now, and this was the first time she'd ventured out at night. He waited until she'd gained a block on him before easing from the shadows and following her.

This area of the city was mostly flats and small businesses. He frowned when it seemed she was walking in the direction of the metro. But she bypassed the public transportation. It didn't take long for him to realize she was going to a local tavern.

He crossed the street, careful to stay out of her sight. No one lingered on the street, and traffic was sparse. He could wait until she had a few drinks and was on her way home, but she might not leave the place alone. Or he could strike now.

Decision made, he moved forward.

Chapter 11

She was proving a point, if only to herself.

Pamela was tired of hiding behind her locked apartment door, as if she was some brainless, helpless female. Just speaking to Twyla had made her feel better. Her sister was digging into the whys and wherefores of one Dmitri Antonio Andropolis—she hadn't even known he had a middle name—and as a side dish to the entree, his half brother, Dylan Justin Pierce.

She and Twyla had talked for a long time. Twyla had pointed out that she'd really done nothing that would cause someone to want to take a contract out on her. The one possibility that her sister had raised seemed more likely the longer she thought about it. It was very possible that Dylan had been overplaying his "someone's trying to kill you" card. She didn't have to think too long and hard to figure out why, either. What better way to get close to her and to keep *her* close than to invent a threat that the big, brave man could protect her from?

So tonight was a test. She was walking to the tavern about a half kilometer from her home, she was going to have a couple of glasses of wine, and then she was going to walk home again.

A whisper of sound behind her sent a shiver down her back. Determined, she pushed the shadow of fear away. Had she ever taken this walk without seeing either rats or cats scurrying in the alley? Not once. Amazing the colors and shadings the brain could provide when it was fuelled by the right accelerant. It was time to leave the tendrils of terror behind. She just needed to prove to herself that she had nothing to be afraid of. *Mind over matter, Pamela. It's just a case of mind over matter.*

An arm snaked around her neck, jerking her back. A blade waved in front of her face, stifling her scream before she could open her mouth.

"Time's up, Pammy." The words, hissed, galvanized her. Fear exploded and was pushed ruthlessly aside. There was no time for fear, just for cold, clear thought. She whimpered once, allowing her unknown attacker to pull her back toward the entrance to the alley she'd just passed. Allowing him to think she was cowed.

"First, you get to hurt. Payback for surviving Philadelphia and for costing me a prime contract. Then, you get to die, bitch."

He'd loosened his hold just a fraction, and that was all she needed. The blade was in front of her face but not pointed at her throat. *His mistake, my good fortune.* She pitched her body forward and to the left. Throwing her right arm up and behind her, the back of her closed fist slammed into his face. She heard the crunch of cartilage, smelled the copper-stench of blood at the same time she tried to grab his weapon arm and execute one of the throws she'd learned in self-defense class.

Her grip failed, and all she managed to do was force him away a few paces as he stumbled, trying to regain his balance. She spun around, facing him, just as his back hit the opposite wall, bouncing him forward, toward her.

"Bitch!" He backhanded her hard with his left hand. *Knee-jerk. Should have used the knife. Another mistake.* Connecting against her left cheek, just under her eye, the force of his blow snapped her head back. Stars swam in front of her face.

"That's one more you get to pay for. I'm going to enjoy hurting you, bitch."

Her attacker's lurid threat sounded too close by far. Her head cleared; her eyes focused, took in his stance. Legs spread for balance, both arms out, and that blade now gripped with purpose.

Oh, shit. He advanced on her slowly, and she had no place to go and no way to safely attack him. *Okay, forget safe.* Her gaze never leaving his, she whipped her t-shirt over her head. By the flicker in his eyes, she knew she'd taken him off balance.

"Wanna play, do you?"

Ignoring his taunt, not caring that she was exposing her breasts in her skimpy bra to his view, she spun her left arm in a circle, effectively wrapping the shirt around her forearm. It wasn't a lot of fabric, but it was all the protection for her arm she had. *Lead with your left; follow through with your right.* Somehow, she didn't think her instructor had just this kind of scenario in mind.

She caught him off guard with a feint to the left and her strike forward. Watching his eyes, she saw that one moment of inattention, that millisecond when his brain tried to catch up with his reality, and she moved.

With her right foot, she kicked him hard, square in the groin.

He went down, and she moved in, intending to boot him in the face. His hand shot out, grabbed her ankle, and pulled.

Ass and elbows smashed into worn cobblestone, and the shock of impact jarred her whole body. Even cursing and in pain, her attacker stumbled to his feet, prepared to lunge. Pamela tried to skitter away backwards on hands and feet, but she was on the ground, hurting and out of time.

"*Son of a bitch.*"

The epithet, the charge from the shadows, startled her. The sound of flesh on flesh, grunts, moans, and curses jumbled in her pain-rattled brain. But she recognized this new voice.

"Dylan, be careful! He has a knife!"

Both men fell to the ground, twisting and rolling, struggling for life and for vengeance. Then the blade rose above them, a steel raptor hovering over prey, waiting for the weakest moment, the weakest man.

The knife plunged. Pamela screamed.

Slowly, one man rose from the stones. The second lay immobile on the ground, knife handle protruding from his chest.

It took her a moment to realize Dylan was kneeling before her, brushing the hair from her face.

"Are you all right?"

His voice was shaking, and when he pulled his hand back, blood trailed down his arm.

"You're bleeding. Where are you hurt?" The red oozing fluid cut through the red haze of her shock.

"Bastard nicked my shoulder."

Not saying another word, Pamela unwound the material from her arm, got to her knees, and pulled back Dylan's shirt.

"Fuck, that stings."

"Quit bitching." She pressed her shirt hard against his shoulder, but her eyes strayed to the body of her attacker. Then another figure loomed at the opening of the alley, and she gasped.

"Pierce!"

"Here." He'd turned his head toward the voice then said to Pamela, "It's okay. He's with me."

The man approached, squatted by the body, felt for a pulse. Then he turned his attention to them. Pamela thought she recognized the man from her trip to the *épicerie* the other day.

"This is Terry Miller, late of Scotland Yard, now a private investigator. An old friend."

Pamela nodded to the man, who said nothing in return but pulled out his cell phone and moved off to the opening of the alley. She turned her attention back to Dylan.

"I thought I left you behind in New York." Now that the adrenalin was wearing off, she began to shiver even as her brain started to function again.

"Did you really think I was going to let you wander the streets of the world alone, when someone was trying to kill you?"

Time, she thought, to begin to accept the truth. "Yeah, about that. I hadn't believed you. But it seems you may have been right."

Her gaze caught Dylan's for a long moment. He reached forward and gently caressed her face.

"We'll talk," he said.

* * * *

Inspector Michaud waited until the doctor had finished dressing Dylan's wound at the hospital before beginning his follow-up interrogation. The attitude of the officer was cordial; that was due in part to the fact that Dylan's friend, Terry, was an investigator known and liked by the Paris *gens d'armes*. The other part had to do with Pamela. She was held in high regard in the small neighborhood where she'd lived the last few years.

"You did not recognize this attacker, then, either of you?"

"I've never seen him before in my life," Pamela said quietly. She was still shivering. One of the nurses had provided her with a cotton top to wear, so he figured her shivering was more from shock than from being cold. Dylan wanted to wrap his arms around her but figured that move wouldn't be appreciated quite yet.

"I have to say the same. Any idea who he is, Inspector?"

"He carried identification, but we are waiting for verification. This was, perhaps, a random attack?"

"No. He knew my name. He was mad that I'd survived his attempts on my life in Philadelphia." Pamela's stark admission sounded hollow, and Dylan guessed she was dealing with the very real knowledge that someone had just tried to kill her. Again.

He gave the inspector details about the two incidents in Philadelphia and gave him the name of his friend on the PPD.

"Mademoiselle Singer, who would want to kill you?"

Dylan watched Pamela's face as she answered the inspector.

"I honestly don't know. I never believed you," she said then, and when she looked at Dylan, he realized, somehow, she was telling the truth. She clearly had no idea who her enemy was. "Since coming home, I'd convinced myself it was just one more lie you had told me."

"*Oui?*"

The tone the inspector used in that one word as he drilled Dylan with his stare was enough to have him squirm in his seat.

"A private disagreement," Pamela said quietly.

"Well, perhaps now that Monsieur Pierce has saved your life, your disagreement can be…mended?"

She gave nothing of her thoughts away when she answered only, "Perhaps."

"That is all for now. I will be in touch with you both tomorrow. If you think of anything more, however insignificant it may seem, you will call. Yes?"

"Of course," Dylan answered for them both.

When the cop left the room, he and Pamela were alone for the first time since arriving at the hospital.

"What do you want from me, Dylan?"

In those seven words, Dylan heard disillusionment and exhaustion. It was getting damn hard not to wrap her in his arms and just hold her.

"From you? Nothing." A lie, but she wasn't ready to hear the truth yet. "For you? I want you safe. In spite of everything, I find I can't leave you alone. I care about you very much. I want to do everything I can to protect you."

"Do you mean in spite of the lies you've told and the game you've played, or in spite of what you *think* I've done?"

When he was slow to answer, she shook her head. "Never mind." She got to her feet. "That was a stupid fucking question."

"Wait." If she walked out now, he'd never get her back. And it did surprise him that, underneath everything, that was the answer to her question. That was what he wanted. That was the only thing that really mattered.

"How about a truce? Someone *is* trying to kill you. I have the resources to find out who and why—and more importantly to see that whoever it is fails. Please, Pamela. Let me help."

She took two steps away from him, her attention fixed outside the small barred window. He wished he could read her, but she was proving adept at closing off her emotions.

"All right. What do we do next?"

* * * *

Peter Abbott put himself on a park bench in an area he knew Sykes frequented. Though he'd be the first to admit he had little in common with the man, they had one thing that bound them. And that one thing was quite possibly going to kill them both.

Sitting alone, slowly tossing crumbs to the pigeons, he'd had to wait only an hour, which was remarkable, really.

"Those birds will get cheeky if you let them, governor," Sykes said as he sat down beside him.

There weren't many people about. Peter waited until a woman and child passed before speaking. "So I've noticed. We have a decision to make." He met Sykes's eyes and knew, in that moment, he wasn't alone in either his fears or his desires. He hoped total honesty would lay the ground-work for a new alliance.

"I want out. I've a business to take over, and I want a life. But with this sword of Damocles, as it were, hanging over my head, I'm screwed. And I'm damned good and tired of feeling like a pawn in a chess game."

"I've been thinking a change in identity might be nice. Only thing is, not knowing who that bloody blighter is, that 'banker,' I can't be sure even that would protect me." Sykes's tone, edged with anger, told Peter all he needed to know. He'd trust him. He didn't, really, have much choice.

"Changing identity isn't an option for me. The Banker's plan has failed. The Singer woman has survived the attempts on her life. Three times, from what I've heard. By now, she'll know someone's out to get her. The chances of success have dropped dramatically."

"Can't say as I'm sorry about that part. I've never had a hand in murder. Didn't want to start at this point in my life."

"Nor I." They sat silently for a moment while the occasional person walked past and the pigeons fought over the bit of seed Peter casually tossed out.

"Is there another way out of this mess? Rather than changing me name and me country?"

"I've been thinking. We're not the only ones who're at risk right now."

"I don't give a frig about Irons. Bastard can hang from The Tower for all I care. "

"I wasn't thinking of him. I'm referring to The Provider – to Danbury. And I was wondering how hard it would be to convince him that *Irons* was about to get talkative with the cops." He looked over at Timmy and had the pleasure of seeing, not only that he understood, but that he thought the idea amusing.

"Well, you're a right clever one, aren't you? Do you think Danbury knows who The Banker is?"

"Perhaps not now, but given the right incentive to find out…" He let the sentence hang.

"Aye. He's wilier than two foxes, that one. He's got his fingers into everything. And I'd bet he'd be grateful for a tip like that."

"That was what I was hoping. He's not one to be played. Can't allow it. It would be bad for business. It'll take me a few days to see my way there so that it'll look normal. But once I've planted that seed…"

"He'll send someone to chat me up, won't he? And I'll be all tight and nervous-like, suspicious, too. Accuse him at first of being in with that wanker, Irons. Make his man work for the scrap."

"Perfect. Once we've set it into motion, there'll be no going back." Peter wasn't sure if he was warning Sykes or just saying it aloud for his own benefit.

"Can't see any reason to go back. Andropolis has been getting more unstable over the years, hasn't he? The heart's gone out of the group, and it's time we all moved on. The way I see it, this is our only shot. We should meet again, see where it's at. Let's say Saturday night, week after next. Black Friar's. This time of year, the place is loaded with tourists. I've a bit of picking in me past, so if anyone's watching, it'll be a natural enough place for me to be. You got some fancy clients you can use?"

"I've been known to go there from time to time on my own. So my appearing there would be normal enough."

Without another word, Sykes moved off. Peter stayed where he was for a few more minutes, just in case he was being observed. He was committed now, no turning back.

He only wished he knew if the step he'd just taken would lead him to freedom—or death.

Chapter 12

"I love what you've done with the place."

Pamela tried not to be amused by Dylan's dry rejoinder. Since she'd heard similar sentiments from both her sisters when they'd visited, she wasn't insulted.

Her space was sparsely furnished, the minimalist approach, she supposed, to living. When she was home, she was working or sleeping. Scanning her great room, such as it was, she turned to Dylan.

"Well, it's not a suite at the Ritz. Which you likely have booked into, I'm sure." She knew she didn't have to say the words. He was a bright cookie. He'd understand her meaning.

"True. But this apartment, as barren of creature comforts as it is, has something that suite lacks. You. Now, if you'd care to throw some things into a bag, we can take our party over there. We have room service there and everything. I'll even guarantee you have your own bedroom—as the penthouse suite offers three."

Oh, he was good. There was the look that had started it all, that earnest, caring look that had shot through all her defenses. She desperately needed time to shore up those weakened ramparts of hers, but she was very much afraid that, for the second time that night, she'd run out of time. "Sorry, I'm in the middle of a job. You want to be so damned close to me, you'll have to make do with this lovely fifties-style sofa for your bed. Allow me to give you the grand tour. There's the kitchen." She pointed to the north corner of the room. "There's the bath." She pointed to the tiny door just off the kitchen. "My bedroom, off limits." She indicated behind and to the right. "My studio"—She pointed behind and to the left—"which is where I'm headed now. Make yourself at home. *Mi casa su casa* and all that crap. Oh, and not only is there no room service, but the cupboards are practically bare. Sorry, wasn't expecting guests."

She hadn't realized until she spun on her heel that she'd been hoping to provoke him into a battle. A good, strong rousing fight might just give her the energy she needed to slap up a temporary wall, at least. And wasn't he the smart one not to give her what she wanted?

"You're going to your studio now? It's after midnight."

His tone, reasonable and concerned, took the starch out of her attitude. "I need to work, Dylan." Closing her eyes, she waited. She hadn't meant to let him see any more pieces of her soul. When she'd left him behind in New York, she was certain that she had indeed left him behind and that she would, in time, get over him.

Having him in the same room—hell, in the same country—just brought the awful truth home.

She was in love with Dylan Pierce. All-the-way in love with the man. And didn't that make her a prize idiot?

When he said nothing more, she entered the studio.

Here she would ground herself. Here she would get hold of her nerves and her emotions. Not about Dylan—there was no getting hold of that—but with the frightening events of this night. With the reality of having fought a man with a knife, and coming so close to dying. The inspector had it exactly right. Dylan had saved her life tonight.

She couldn't think about it anymore right now. She needed to work. The work would ground her.

Getting out her tools, she set about removing the painting from its frame. Then she carefully removed the protective backing board. The back of the canvas showed its age but was sound. Cleaning it would be the first step in restoration.

For now, she carefully set the painting on her easel. At her computer, she brought up the grid she'd made earlier. Her clipboard was ready. Turning on the brighter overhead light, she took up her infrared scope. Beginning at the lower left-hand corner of the painting, she got to work.

This was what soothed her. The rhythm of the work, of opening her senses to a creation from centuries past, playing sleuth to discover the total story of the art allowed her to step away from her day-to-day reality. This was her constant, her touchstone.

While she focused her mind on what had kept her grounded since that first moment so many years before in Arthur Kensington's gallery in Philadelphia, her heart, body, and soul would come to grips with the fact that her life was in jeopardy, and the only person she could count on to help in the here and now was Dylan Pierce.

* * * *

He didn't follow her. He was in her apartment, and for right this minute, that would have to be enough.

Dylan figured letting Pamela have her space was the wisest thing he could do—not to mention the opportunity it would allow him to check in with several of his contacts.

Terry was the first.

"What have you got for me?" Dylan kept his voice low as he spoke on his cell phone. Pacing over to the front windows that looked down over the quiet street, he focused all his attention on the investigator.

"Billy O'Reilly is well known to the London constabulary," Terry said.

Dylan had asked the inspector if their assailant had been identified. Terry had done a quick search of the man just after he'd called the police and jotted down the details. He'd bet Terry had the scoop on the thug before the Paris police did.

"Petty crimes, mostly," Terry continued, "but a year ago they think he graduated up to murder for hire. Small contracts, small players. They brought him in for questioning a couple of times, but lack of evidence and blah, blah, blah."

"And recently he moved up the food chain, apparently. Had to be some contract to move him overseas and back again. Do they show any known associates?"

"A couple. Some guy named Asher, who hasn't been seen for a couple of weeks. Heathrow shows both him and O'Reilly flying to New York about that time, with only O'Reilly returning at the end of last week."

"Keep on it, Terry, please. Maybe one of his buddies knows who his latest employer was."

His next call was to his hotel. Speaking to the night manager, he collected his messages—Dmitri had left one, as had Hunter Symington—and informed the man he wasn't going to be back until the next day.

He was hoping he could talk Pamela into coming with him to gather his stuff. It seemed pretty clear to him that she was going to hunker down and burrow in her own nest. All things considered, he couldn't blame her. But there was no way in hell he was going to let her stay here alone while he made his way to the center of the city.

Dylan contemplated the two messages he'd received. There was only an hour's difference between Paris and Athens. Telling himself that Dmitri was likely in the midst of an evening with friends, he opted to call Hunter. As his call went through, he tried not to think about the fact that he'd avoided talking to his brother since his trip to the States.

"Dylan, there you are. Paris now, is it? Still chasing the Singer woman?"

"I'm not giving up. What do you have for me?"

"Not much more, I'm sorry to say. I do have the address of her flat in Paris. Do you have a pen?"

It was on the tip of his tongue to tell Hunter not to bother. But then he'd only have to explain what the hell he was doing, and he'd rather not do that quite yet. Mainly, of course, because he had no idea *what* he was doing.

"Shoot."

He listened as the man then ran through a litany of Pamela Singer's employment history.

"Started at that gallery—and likely the gallery owner—before she even graduated high school. I'd say the woman was a born operator."

"It certainly looks that way," Dylan agreed.

"Not too many details on her time over in Jolly Old after she raked in money from Carmichael McRae's estate. We already knew about the position that fell through with the Met in New York. Shortly after that is when she went back to London. She *did* stay with Patrick Mulchaey at his estate in Wiltshire, Barrister's Crossing, for the better part of a year. Don't know if you've ever heard of him or not, but one of his great-grandfathers started a shipping company sometime in the mid eighteen hundreds. Successive generations proved very adept at making money. Anyway, her making a place for herself there was a coup, since the man's known as a total recluse. Reports show him as still hale and hearty, but it appears she netted a nice check for her time and trouble when she moved on."

"Is any of this a matter of public record?"

"Well, the bequests she's received from Kensington and from McRae certainly are, and I imagine any other money she's received can be traced through bank records."

"All right, thanks, Hunter."

"There is just one more thing, Dylan. Dmitri has been trying to get in touch with you. Apparently, your father has sent out word to all and sundry that they are not to tell him where you are."

"I'll give him a call in the morning."

"Best to make it after noon hour. I spoke to him a little while ago, and he was well on his way to a five-star drunk."

"Thanks."

For a moment, thoughts of his brother swamped him. Dmitri had been drinking a lot lately. Dylan suppressed his guilt. He'd spent considerable emotional coin trying to ensure that his brother was treated fairly and well. But Dmitri was a grown man of forty, and right at this point in time, Dylan's focus lay elsewhere. He'd deal with his brother and do what he could to smooth things over with the family, but later. He slipped his cell phone back in his pocket and sat for a long minute, looking at the details he'd written down as Hunter had been speaking.

The bare details of Pamela's life seemed damning. But they were at odds with the woman she appeared to be and the things he'd come to know about her—and certainly didn't mesh with her living conditions. According to everything he knew, she had to be sitting on a sizeable fortune. Looking around the loft apartment that was her home—though he knew the price of it must have been steep—it was hard to tell she had money. All her furnishings looked used, and there was really nothing of value among her possessions. He'd seen no signs of drug use, she didn't even smoke, and she drank sparingly. Usually people who pursued high-risk behavior—such as conning older men out of vast chunks of money—had equally high-risk habits or addictions.

From what he'd observed so far, Pamela had none. Shit, the lady didn't even buy things when she went shopping.

Checking his watch, he was surprised to see an hour had passed. There'd been no sound from the studio; neither had Pamela surfaced from there since she'd gone in.

Curious, he decided to snoop. Only a few steps were needed to take him to the open door of the space. The room appeared almost as large as the sitting room he was in. Leaning against the doorframe, he watched.

Pamela seemed completely absorbed in her work. She'd peer at the painting for what seemed long minutes at a time through some sort of scope. Then she'd stop, make notes on her clip-board, and then return to her inspection.

Curiosity overruled discretion.

"What are you doing?"

"Preliminary examination."

Well that was certainly informative. "Which means?"

He couldn't prevent his smile when she sighed heavily. "In this first step, I'm using the infrared to look for signs that the painting has been worked on before. With careful inspection, I can see where, in the past, others have attempted to repair damage—sometimes just damage to the paint and sometimes where the original canvas has been compromised. Before I do any work myself, I make a complete report to the owner, using a grid to illustrate where on the painting previous intrusions have occurred. I also make recommendations on what needs to be done. The owner then approves or alters that list. This one's not too bad." With the last sentence, her voice had softened. By her tone and the way she looked at the art, he understood that *here* was her passion, her addiction. "There're a few places that need a healing touch. But mostly, this darling just needs some TLC and a good cleaning."

"How long will it take?"

"Not very long at all, only a few weeks." She straightened then, looked at him over her shoulder. Her expression sober, she said, "It's late. I'll give you some linen for the sofa."

"I'll sleep when you sleep."

"I'm going to have a soak in my tub first. This evening's entertainment has left me sore."

She turned to him then, and he got the first look at her with her face under the brighter lights of her studio. The discoloration spiked his temper. It was all he could do to make his approach slow, his touch gentle as he caressed her left cheek.

"You didn't tell me that bastard laid hands on you. You're going to have a black eye."

"You were a little busy when you got there. Afterward, it seemed moot. The bastard was dead." She looked away from him, and he sensed her discomfort.

He waited patiently for her to turn back to him.

"I didn't thank you" she said quietly when she had.

"You were too busy using your t-shirt to sop up my blood."

She actually flinched at that. *Ah, good, she cares more than she's letting on.*

"One or both of us could have died tonight. I'm having a hard time coming to grips with the reality of that, with knowing that someone hates me enough to want me dead. So thank you, Dylan. Thank you for saving my life and at the peril of your own." Her touch, when she reached out to caress his bandaged shoulder, was gentle.

The expression in her eyes when she finally let her gaze meet his was complete vulnerability. He could move now, he realized. He could pull her close, kiss her, and love her. And she'd be his for the night.

Or he could be smart and begin to build something that would last beyond this one night.

Sometimes being smart was pure hell.

"You're welcome. Let's turn in. We can regroup and try to figure things out, in the morning."

Chapter 13

The café featured excellent beignets and wonderful café au lait. That, coupled with the fact that it was *not* her apartment, helped Pamela relax after a fitful night's sleep. Dylan had chosen a back corner of the eatery, sitting with his back to the wall, placing her on his left.

It was a strange sensation, having someone watch over her so aggressively. Normally, she'd be the first one to assert her independence and her ability to take care of herself. But she'd never had anyone try to kill her before. She was more than willing to let someone else call the shots. It was even stranger that someone was Dylan Pierce. Another reason to be glad they were in a public place. She wouldn't jump his bones here.

Being in such close proximity to him was wreaking havoc on her decision to consider him passé. She hadn't completely forgiven him his deceptions. But the edge of her anger was becoming harder to hold on to.

"Our friend last night was a two-bit thug by the name of Billy O'Reilly." Dylan's voice was quiet as he began to speak. She noticed that he was watchful of their surroundings. The bizarre thought crossed her mind that she wouldn't be surprised to hear thriller-movie theme music begin to play in the background. She would have laughed if the circumstances weren't so serious. *Lack of sleep.* She focused on Dylan.

"He was born in London, and at the time of his death, at the ripe old age of twenty-eight, possessed a rap sheet of some merit and aspirations for bigger and better credits in the world of crime—apparently."

"Aspirations that are doomed to never be brought to fruition," she said.

"Thank God."

"Do you have any idea who hired him?"

"None. Terry's still working on it. I also have my friend on the Philadelphia Police Department looking into things."

"If we're pretty certain the man behind the attempts in Philadelphia is O'Reilly, what is there left to find out back there?" Pamela didn't even have a history of reading murder mysteries, so she had no idea what steps the police would take or what all could possibly be involved in arranging for a "hit." She shivered just thinking the word. Then an idea occurred to her. "You mean he followed me here from there?"

"Oh, it's worse than that. He followed you there from here, first. He'd been to the States only twice in his life that Terry has been able to discern. O'Reilly was based in London."

"I haven't been to London—well, I went there for a weekend with your brother, but other than that, I've not been in England for a couple of years." Pamela could see Dylan struggling with himself. He wanted to ask her about everything he'd heard. He wanted answers to the questions he had about her.

Damned if she would assuage his curiosity. In the first place, none of it was really any of his business. In the second place, she felt a strange kind of reluctance to share the details of her past with him. If they were going to have any kind of a future, then he needed to accept her for the person she was, here and now, warts…and reputations…and all.

Since when have I been thinking of having a future with Dylan Pierce? She wanted to deny that train of thought, to chalk it up as well to a lack of sleep and general pissiness at being targeted by a killer.

She couldn't, however, lie to herself. Being in love with the man, there was naturally a part of her that tended to think of a future and happy-ever-after. Right at this moment, though, she didn't want to think about any of that, because whether it could be or not was anyone's guess.

"Could you have an enemy in London?"

She supposed it was the least obtrusive way of asking for details of her past. She bought herself a few seconds by taking a bite of her beignet and chewing slowly.

"I can't see how." This was nothing but the truth. Carmichael had lived in London and Paris, but his niece and nephew both resided in the States, despite the fact they were often on this side of the pond. She really didn't think either of them would have anything to do with this, anyway. There'd be no profit in her death for either of them. That thought reminded her of some of her conversation with her sister.

"No one would gain."

"Gain?" She could see by Dylan's expression he wasn't following her train of thought.

"If I were to die. I have a will, of course. It names my sisters equally, and if you try to tell me one of them—"

He picked up her hand, stroked the back of it in what she recognized as a soothing gesture. "It isn't always about gain. There are other motives for murder. Sometimes it's about payback." His level stare told her that's what he thought lay behind this trouble. "And sometimes, it's just pure malice."

Dylan released her hand, and she immediately picked up her coffee cup. There was only one person who came to mind when he'd said the words "payback" and "malice." But she doubted very much he'd consider for one moment the villain they were after could be his very own brother.

* * * *

Dylan kept Pamela in his peripheral vision as the cab wound its way toward his hotel. The Carstairs Elysées Paris, located close to the Arc de Triumphe, was one of the first European hotels his grandmother had acquired. Built in the late eighteen hundreds, its massive structure resembled an enormous manor house. Inside, furnishings and tapestries called to a bygone era, and the guest could feel his fifteen hundred Euros per night tariff was well justified.

Or so the company line went.

He was having a hell of a time reconciling the Pamela he knew with the woman he'd heard about from both Dmitri and Hunter. That woman would have expected Dylan to have hired a chauffeur-driven car to take them where they needed to go.

This one had headed for the metro station before he'd forestalled her and arranged for a cab instead.

"I've never been beyond the lobby and restaurant in this place," Pamela said as they got out of the cab at the hotel entrance. Then she turned to him. "How can you conscience bilking people for so much just to *sleep* here?"

Dylan fought his smile. "Don't ever let my granny hear you say that. I'll have you know this hotel enjoys one of the highest occupancy rates of all the ones we own. 'Luxury for the discerning traveller.'"

"I guess packaging and marketing are everything," she said quietly as they moved through the double doors being held open by the uniformed doormen.

"No, that's only part of it. The rest is location, location, location."

He wished he could talk her into bringing a few things and staying here with him. If they were still lovers, he knew he'd have no problem convincing her. But they weren't—yet—and he could certainly understand her desire for "home turf." Nearly being killed stole the sense of control from a person. Staying in your own home gave at least an illusion of control back.

"I just want to gather my messages, some clothes, and my laptop."

"You can do hotel business from my flat?"

There was a part of him that wanted very much to be as tight-lipped about the details of his life as she was being about her own. But he doubted that would serve anything but to stroke his pride.

Shaking his head, he led her toward the elevator and said quietly, "While I do occasionally step in and handle things for Granny, mostly I work for the other family business." Her blank look just raised more questions in his mind. "The Moerae Corporation. Shipping, import/export, real estate."

He found it odd there was no light of recognition in her eyes. Unlike himself, who sometimes wore several different hats, being a VP for Moerae was the only title Dmitri held.

"Moerae? As in The Three Fates of mythology?"

He couldn't prevent his wide smile. "The same. Grandfather Leandros, my mother's father, lost practically everything during World War Two and then discovered a sunken treasure just outside Greek territorial waters. He said his second chance was pure fate."

Pamela shook her head, and in the gesture, Dylan read irony.

"What?"

"Have you *read* any Greek mythology?"

"I'll remind you that my mother's name is Maria Leandros Andropolis Pierce. You can take that as a yes."

"Three more heartless women you'll never meet. Had to figure those bitches were at the bottom of my trouble."

Dylan found he really had nothing to say to that.

* * * *

The penthouse suite reminded her a little of Patrick Mulchaey's palatial home in Wiltshire. Here, she thought, was the best Europe had to offer in furnishings, tapestries, styling, and ambience.

Dylan had been right, of course. The suite did have three bedrooms. Maybe she was being a bit childish, insisting they stay at her modest flat instead of here, in the lap of luxury.

Except living on Dylan Pierce's dime felt entirely too uncomfortable, all things considered. She wanted to maintain the right to toss him out on his sorry ass if she had to.

"I've got a message here to call Michael. The friend I told you about in Philly?"

"Ah. The cop."

"That's the one. So why not just make yourself comfortable while I—" Dylan stopped when a phone rang. It was her cell phone. Pulling it out of her jeans pocket, she held it up to show him. Looking at the call display, relief flooded her when she recognized Twyla's number. Moving off to the other side of the sitting room, she answered it as Dylan sat down at the antique desk to call the States on the hotel phone.

"Hey, little sister." Pamela said.

"Hey, yourself. I wasn't sure if it was a good time to call or not. I know you can be anal when you're working."

Pamela smiled. It was really good to hear her sister's voice. "Well, as it happens, I'm not working at the moment."

"Good. Okay, first off, I haven't been able to find anything on Pierce. He's got no arrests, no suspected of, and no real bad gossip. Graduated magna cum laude from Harvard Business School, started out his career working for his grandmother as a bellhop at her flagship hotel—the one in San Francisco. No shady stories from business contacts he's stabbed in the back, because the word is he's a straight shooter. Loyal, though from your experience with him I'd say not completely housebroken. Good thing you decided to take that puppy back to the pound."

"Hmm."

"Oh, oh. A hmm from you can mean only one thing. Don't tell me you're giving that slime bucket a second chance?"

Pamela smiled. Her sister was loyal, too, sometimes beyond reason. Anyone ever did either herself or Alba wrong, that person was on a par with a lump of dog do-do for the rest of their natural lives and beyond, as far as Twyla was concerned.

"Long story, but he more or less saved my life last night."

"What the hell? What happened?"

"I'll fill you in shortly. What else did you find out?"

"Okay, if he saved your life, now he's my hero. I have a pedestal around somewhere. I'll dig it out. His half brother, on the other hand, hasn't a heroic bone in his body. On him, I found all sorts of crap. Everything from being suspended from three different private schools for bullying and total disregard for authority, to the latest. It seems he's been fired from the family business. Word on the street is he helped himself to a half a mill from petty cash."

Pamela frowned. Turning her back on Dylan, who was just being put through to his cop friend, she said, "That must be the half million Dylan accused me of taking."

"Well he's an asshole if thinks for one minute that you would ever—"

"We're in agreement there." It *really* was good to hear from her sister.

"Anyway, there is some gossip that Andropolis has crossed the wrong people. Plus, he's about run through all his trust fund money and current company dividends. Speculation that a deal he thought was going to pay big went south about six months ago. Any clues there?"

Little things were beginning to come together for her. Dmitri had seemed fascinated with her work and very concerned with her security arrangements. From the tone of Twyla's question, she guessed her sister was thinking along the same lines.

"Okay, thanks. I don't think Dylan has a clue about any of that."

"And you're not going to tell him?"

Pamela thought about that for a moment. She and Dylan were a long way off from that point where trust ebbed and flowed between them. Twyla's investigation had only confirmed what she already knew. Loyalty was one of Dylan's finest traits. When he did learn the truth about his brother—and if things were spiraling down for Dmitri as they seemed to be, he would find out sooner rather than later—he would be devastated. Maybe she'd be there then to offer him a shoulder. But would she go out of her way to tell him the truth about Dmitri? "Not in this lifetime," she said to Twyla.

"No, I suppose you wouldn't. So, what happened last night?"

In as few words as possible, Pamela filled her in, including the identity of the would-be assassin. She cringed when her sister swore, loud and long.

"Two words, P.J., *Pepper spray*." Twyla always called her P.J. when she was annoyed or excited.

"I don't think that stuff is legal to carry."

"I don't give a rat's ass if it's legal or not. You get some."

"Okay."

"Who am I kidding? You won't get some. Keep your phone charged up and keep me in the loop."

Pamela hung up and slipped her phone back into her pocket. She turned to face Dylan and her stomach dropped when she saw the look of despair on his face.

She went to him even as he was finishing up his call.

"We'll both be there as soon as possible, Michael. I'll call when we're in the air."

"What's wrong?"

Dylan had placed the receiver down and closed his eyes. She waited, her belly tightening with dread.

"One more thing I did and didn't confess to you. I'm sorry. I believed what Dmitri had told me and the information I received from a couple of other sources. It seemed you had a pattern, a 'type,' if you will, of man you liked to…associate with. So I arranged for you to meet just such a man."

"Meet who?" Pamela asked, but she already knew. And she was really afraid she knew why Dylan was so upset.

"Eric Llewellyn. Michael just informed me he's been murdered…and we're both considered 'persons of interest' in the case by the Philadelphia police."

Chapter 14

Michael Parker didn't fit Pamela's idea of a police detective or a friend of Dylan's. *It's the glasses.* Big black frames swamped a face that seemed unassuming, almost nerd-like. Tall and thin, the man practically swam in his suit jacket, which was an olive green and really didn't do anything nice for his complexion.

It was Pamela's first visit to a police headquarters building. She wasn't sure what she had expected—maybe a large, open room with men in shirtsleeves, some interviewing sleazy suspects, all the while sweating in the oppressive heat of summer while the smell of burnt coffee coated everything.

What she found was a clean, modern workplace, much like any other place of business. Lieutenant Parker had his own small office, and on arrival, she and Dylan were escorted to it.

"I'm not going to show you the crime scene photographs," Parker said after they'd been seated. "I will tell you that Eric Llewellyn died badly. I'm sorry, Dylan. I know he was a friend of yours."

"You said that Pamela and I were 'persons of interest.'"

"Yeah." At this point, he sat back. Taking off his glasses, he plucked a tissue from the box on the credenza behind his desk and began to clean them.

"For the record, I'd like you to tell me your whereabouts—both of you—on Saturday, August second. I'm particularly interested in the hours between eleven in the morning and two in the afternoon."

Pamela often wondered how ordinary people could be expected to recall where they were and what they had been doing a week or more in the past. She'd never been one to hang onto those kinds of details.

"Ah yes, I remember last month, on the twentieth. It was a sunny day with a slight breeze, so I decided to go for a walk along the river." Those sorts of reflections would never be hers. Unless something had happened to make the day stand out in big bold letters in her memory.

Getting shot at from a passing car while walking along a popular Philadelphia street had certainly done that.

"That was the day we went to Rittenhouse Square…"

"And got shot at," Dylan finished dryly. "It happened just before lunch. I'm afraid I don't recall the name of the officer who took our statements…"

It was Pamela's turn to finish his sentence. "I do. It was Officer Markel. But I don't remember what precinct or division or whatever it was he was with."

"We went directly from there over to the emergency room at Jefferson, via hotel limousine. Doctor Theodore Samuelson met us as soon as we arrived. I think we were there about a half hour or so. Is that good enough?"

Parker slipped his glasses back on. "Yeah, that puts you both in the clear with regard to Mr. Llewellyn's death. Turns out it was a good thing you contacted me before you left for England. I actually took the trouble to check that you *were* both documented as being where I'd known you to be. Which means, my friend, you are in one hell of a deep mess."

"I'm getting that impression," Dylan said.

"I'm afraid I don't understand. If you know we had nothing to do with Mr. Llewellyn's death, how are we in a mess?" At that moment, Pamela wished Twyla was with her. Her sister had a lot more knowledge of cops and procedures and all things criminal than she did. Twyla had, in fact, a keen understanding of how some criminal minds worked, which, considering her profession, was an asset.

All Pamela knew was how to tell a Monet from a Matisse. Not terribly useful information under the current circumstances.

"First, why not tell us why you had us listed as 'persons of interest'?" He reached over for her hand, and Pamela let him have it. A friend of his had been murdered, and she already understood Dylan well enough to know he felt guilty as hell about that.

"We found your business card in the Vic—sorry, in Mr. Llewellyn's pocket, Dylan. And there was a notation in his day planner about a lunch meeting with you, scheduled on the day he died. I sent the book in to the crime lab, because I had a feeling *that* notation was not in his hand."

"No, we had no appointment to meet for lunch."

It seemed that Dylan's statement merely confirmed what the Lieutenant already knew.

"Now, Ms. Singer, on to you. We received a tip that led us to the discovery of Mr. Llewellyn's body on Sunday evening, the evening after he was murdered."

"After I'd already left for Paris."

"Correct. Wise move on your part, by the way, informing Officer Markel of your departure. Anyway, the tip came from one of my men's long-time snitches, and at the time, the information he had seemed solid. The snitch had been 'searching for opportunities,'" Parker read from a sheet of paper. He looked up at her then. "The man was a two-bit thief. He happened to be just by Mr. Llewellyn's second-story balcony. He swears he overheard a roaring argument between a young woman and the older man. That the woman then picked up what appeared to be a fireplace poker and struck the man, repeatedly. The snitch waited until Sunday night to report the matter, as that, apparently, was when his conscience kicked in."

"You said was."

Pamela looked over at Dylan. He returned her look then turned his attention back to the cop. "You said he *was* a two-bit thief."

"You're sharp as ever. I said was, because he's gone missing. Not before identifying Ms. Singer—by photo and by name—as Mr. Llewellyn's assailant."

"Does the snitch have any friends or known associates?"

"As of yesterday, when he couldn't be located, we've been looking. But now you see why I said you're in the middle of a big mess."

Dylan looked even more anguished. She knew she was missing the point and didn't care if they thought she was stupid.

"I still don't understand."

"The reason the snitch is missing is that he can identify the real killer, a killer who knew enough *after* the fact to understand his attempt at framing you wasn't going to work," Dylan said. "And he knew that, because whoever is behind all of this has been monitoring us. He knew we had an alibi for the time of the killing. Which means Eric was killed *because* of us."

"You have a killer on your ass, Dylan," Lieutenant Parker confirmed. "You need to figure out what you're going to do about that."

* * * *

Eric would still be alive if it wasn't for me. That thought had taken up center stage in Dylan's thoughts and would not be dislodged. He stood just inside the door of the penthouse suite of the Carstairs Philadelphia hotel, key card dangling from his hand, and for the moment, at least, had no earthly idea what he was going to do next.

Outside the tall floor-to-ceiling glass, dusk had fallen and the lights of Camden, New Jersey began to come on across the Delaware River.

He felt Pamela come up to him and nearly shivered with hunger when her hand rubbed his back lightly.

"Do you want me to order dinner from room service?"

Her question brought him out of his self-pitying fog. He blinked and then turned to her.

"I'm sorry. I never even asked you. You'll probably want your own room. I can arrange…"

He stopped speaking when, without words, she closed the distance between them and put her arms around him.

"Why?" He wanted so badly to latch onto her, to hold her close and never let her go. There was no logic in that desire, and he didn't care anymore that it was so. There remained just one tiny scrap of pride in him that forced him to ask, "Because you feel sorry for me?"

"No. Because I care. In spite of everything, I care about you, Dylan Pierce. More, I'm afraid, than is probably good for me."

She'd echoed his words. A strangled sound, half laugh and half sob, escaped his throat. And then he was holding her the way he'd wanted to hold her since the night before last. He was holding her, and it seemed that everything in his world came right with this embrace.

He pulled back, framed her face with his hands. There was so much he needed to say to her, if only he could sort out the thoughts from the jumbled mess his mind had become. She returned his look, her own eyes filled with need and confusion.

Now wasn't the time to talk. Now was for touching, for feeling, for giving, and yes, for taking.

He lowered his lips to hers and plundered. She held the secret to life, the nectar that would sustain him, and he gorged himself on her. Her arms convulsing around his neck, her fingers shaking, raking through his hair, told him of her own need and her own passion.

He lifted her without lifting his mouth from hers. As his tongue drank and danced, as her flavor seeped into his blood, he carried her to his bed. Fingers forgot finesse as he opened buttons and zippers and clasps and stripped her bare. Heat rose from her flesh in waves that warmed the frozen parts of his soul. When she struggled to remove the last of the cloth covering his body, he helped her. Then he laid her on the bed and followed her down.

Gentler now, his lips sipped and tasted her as his hands explored and his soul yearned for hers. She was soft and strong, sweet and pliant and demanding all at the same time. Eager to reacquaint himself with her body, her taste, as if their separation had been months instead of only days, he trailed his tongue down her neck, swirled around one pebbled nipple. When she arched her back to give him more of her, he drew the hard bud into his mouth, suckled strongly.

The taste of her soothed and aroused. Her hands, stroking his back, then up, fingers splaying into his hair, comforted and stimulated. It seemed right, somehow, that she could be all things, do all things. No confusion here, no second thoughts or doubts or reservations. Just perfect communication, perfect need. She suited him. They suited each other.

When she lifted up, rising above him, he sprawled on the bed. She stretched his arms out and he left them in that pose of surrender, but he gave up nothing.

Her mouth on his neck, her lithe and supple flesh straddling his as she sipped and explored his flavor became a salve that healed all wounds. The caress of her hair, trailing down his chest, then lower, compelled a groan from deep within him.

Her tongue and lips kissing, tasting, and *finally* taking his engorged cock into her mouth thrilled and humbled.

Unable to remain passive, he reached out, one hand in her hair, entwining his fingers in the strands as he guided her, controlled her in her worship of him. Hormones raged and need spiraled. A second hand joined the first, demanding more. Demanding all.

He felt her give way, understood that she relinquished everything to him in that moment. Civilization stripped from him, he grunted, as if that was the only speech he could make as he thrust his penis in and out of her mouth, taking absolute and complete control, his focus only on his own satiation.

He couldn't stop the spasms that came from the very depth of his being, couldn't ease his actions as he jerked and pushed into her again and again. She rode him, capturing his seed, swallowing it, taking everything he had to give her. Taking all that he was.

Quivering, shivering, the orgasm faded, and all that remained was the gentle pull of her mouth and the exquisite caress of her hands as she stroked his thighs and legs.

* * * *

"Come here," his words penetrated the sensual haze that had devoured her, even as she'd devoured his semen. She had no time to respond, for he was pulling her up gently, enfolding her in his arms.

"Did I hurt you? I never want to hurt you again."

"You didn't. You couldn't, not here, not like this." She burrowed into his arms as they surrounded her, drank up his heat as it saturated her.

How could she have thought she could resist him? She loved him. He was her mate, her other half. He'd been hurting, the wound to his heart deep and desperate. She could no more resist the need in him to be healed than she could the need in herself to succor. She didn't know if they had a future beyond the situation that had caught them fast. She only knew that, for as long as she could, she would be with him, her heart tied to his heart, her fate bound to his fate.

"I met Eric the summer I went to work for my grandmother in San Francisco," Dylan said softly against her hair.

Pamela stroked her hand across Dylan's chest. The sound of his voice, deep and rich and under her ear did strange things to her heart.

Inhaling a shaky breath, he continued. "He was attending a writers' conference at the hotel. He was a history professor from a small college in New York, but he had, he said, the soul of an author."

"He reminded me of a teacher," she said softly. "He seemed like a very nice man."

"He was. It seems like those dozen or so years ago happened in a flash. We connected, and despite the differences in our ages, became good friends. He'd been widowed a year when we met. He and his wife, Paula never had any children."

"I'm sorry you lost him, Dylan."

He fell silent for a while, but his hand caressing her, shoulder to hip, assured her he was only thinking, not sleeping. He played his fingers across the small of her back and stroked the crescent-shaped birthmark there.

"Have I told you that I really like this?"

"A time or two. I hated it, growing up. I always wore a one-piece bathing suit, because I didn't want it to show."

"It's beautiful."

"Thank you." They fell silent for a moment, and Pamela focused on stroking his chest.

"I want to love you," he whispered. When he moved, gently laying her on her back, she slipped her arms around his neck and kissed him gently.

"I want to give you everything that you just gave to me." His voice whisper soft, he returned the favor and kissed her. "I want to give you everything."

"I want that, too. But first I want to have a nice long bath. Then I want to eat something totally expensive from room service."

She desperately wanted her gift to him to remain just that. To bathe, to eat, and then return to this bed would be like raising the curtain on act two.

Looking in his eyes, she thought he understood her intention. His kiss, soft and chaste on her forehead, confirmed it.

"The tub here is big enough for two," he said. His smile, easy and boyish, was nearly clear of shadows.

"So it is. Will you come and bathe with me?"

He caressed her face, the most loving touch she'd ever felt.

"Yes."

Chapter 15

Arousal shot her from sleep.

In the last heartbeat before waking, she'd dreamt of him. His face, anguish and determination blazing from his eyes, had been obscured by distance and a stormy sea. She sang, hoping her song would guide him, realizing too late that the melody she offered blinded him to the perilous rocks he approached.

"Dylan!"

"Yes, love?"

Humor laced his voice as the vibration of his words and his heated breath caressed her feminine flesh, taking her higher.

Reaching down between her legs, she stroked his head, inhaling sharply when he nipped her labia lightly with his teeth.

"Women have an advantage over men. We're restricted in the number of orgasms we can achieve in any given period of time. Your kind doesn't have that same restriction." He followed that provocative statement by taking her clit into his mouth and sucking. He let it go after only a moment. "How many can you have in the next hour, I wonder?"

Sucking that sensitive bud again, he slid fingers into her, stroking slowly. Her hands flexed, digging into his scalp as the first waves crashed through her. Hot, shivery, they bathed her in rapture so sharp she wondered how she would survive it. On and on, the pleasure reached every fiber of her being. Nipples hardening, back arching, she fought for breath.

"One."

Feeling the word more than hearing it, she tossed her head back and forth, meaning to tell him that one was more than enough.

She deluded herself. Reaching up, one masculine hand cupped and squeezed her left breast, while lips and tongue teased and stroked, over, around, inside her pussy. Electric shocks snapped and crackled over her intimate flesh, abrading it to the very edge of tolerance. And then arousal, reborn, relaxed her muscles, opened her intimate passage, moisture readying her to receive whatever gift he offered. Thoughts incoherent, speech impossible, she could only groan in need as her body reached higher, then higher still. He splayed her wider, and she didn't care. All that she was became his as he sucked and licked and plunged.

He played a finger slowly from her swollen, needy clit down across her opening, dipping into her moisture while resisting the lips that flexed as if to grab, stroked down lower, finally rubbing back and forth across her anus.

"Oh, God!" This orgasm ripped her from reality, catapulting her into an otherworld of pulsing, writhing pleasure. This she couldn't control, couldn't manage. It lived, thrived, soared, and she was helpless within its force, could only surrender to its power.

"Two."

Pamela whimpered. Dylan chuckled. Then nothing existed in her world but the touch of him, the heat and the strength and the will of him, as he nuzzled his face against her, blew heated breath upon her, and began again.

* * * *

Knowing he could reduce his woman to a quivering, totally sated state gave a man a sense of real power. *And an even stronger desire to keep her safe.* Dylan ruminated on those facts as the room-service waiter wheeled the table into the suite and went about setting out their breakfast. He was about to go get Pamela from the bedroom when she emerged. The phone rang.

"Pierce."

"You haven't forgotten the charity ball in London tomorrow night?" That lightly accented sentence, spoken with just the right tone of confidence, put a smile on Dylan's face.

"Mother. Is that tomorrow night?"

Her laughter came, predicted and missed. It had been more than three weeks since he'd spoken to her—the last time being just before he left for Philadelphia and his quest.

"Darling, you know it is tomorrow night. If you can't make it, tell me now, and I'll see if I can drag your father away from his sailboat. Of course, he may not forgive you for a while, since he hates dress-up affairs."

Dylan had completely forgotten the gala reception and dance to fund cancer research. It was a cause his mother supported, having lost her own mother to the disease. He turned to look at Pamela, who had just closed the door behind the waiter. Her smile was tentative, as if she wondered if she should give him privacy.

They'd come back to this city because of the death of his friend. He had intended to somehow get them over to London, because he had the feeling the source of their trouble lay there. This reminder of familial duty was just the reason he needed.

"I have a matter to finish dealing with here, but I should be clear in time."

"Yes, I know." Her voice took on the soothing tone he recalled so well from his childhood. It still had the power to ease his heart. "I'm so sorry to hear about Eric. He was murdered? Have they caught the killer?"

"The police are working on it, following all leads."

"And you had to speak to them personally."

"Well, I had been in Philadelphia the day he died, and we were friends. They just wanted to dot their i's and cross their t's." He watched Pamela tilt her head to the side and knew that she understood he was taking some pains not to mention her to his mother.

"Then may I presume you will attend the gala? And that your new lady friend will be attending with you?"

Clever mother. Why was he always surprised by the depth and breadth of her knowledge when it came to her youngest son?

"You may." And then, looking at the woman who waited quietly just there across the room, said, "Her name is Pamela."

"Perhaps you'll bring your Pamela to Athens, and your father and I can meet her. In the meantime, I know you well enough to understand your attempt at discretion. My lips are sealed."

"I love you, Mother."

"And I you, my son. Keep safe."

"I *told* you there would be gossip if you groped me in the lobby."

Pamela's light-hearted banter as he hung up the phone was a gift, letting him off the hook. Walking over to her, he slipped his arms around her but didn't close the distance.

"I wasn't trying to keep you a secret. I just—"

"Dylan, even without the attempts on my life, this entire situation is complicated."

"Thank you."

"You're welcome. Now let's eat. I'm starving."

"Busy night," he couldn't help but comment, laughing when she actually blushed. He poured her some orange juice.

"There was a message waiting for me this morning, left with the front desk. Michael wants us to stop by before we leave town."

"Anything new?"

"The message didn't say."

"We're in the clear, aren't we? He really doesn't think we had anything to do with Eric's death?"

The wave of guilt nearly swamped him. The touch of her hand on his caught his attention. How amazing that it would have a similar effect, only stronger, as that gentle tone of his mother's.

She brought his hand to her lips and kissed it lightly. Then she said, "This is dicey ground, between us. There are issues we've not resolved yet. I think they're going to have to be put on hold until we know what's going on. I won't talk to you about any of it. Except to say this: whatever you did, it was out of love for your brother. It's not your fault Eric is dead. It's the fault of whoever murdered him."

He gripped her hand, accepting the comfort she offered, knowing it was likely more than he deserved. "Thank you for that. And to answer your question, yes, we're in the clear. So there must have been some development in the case he wants us to know about."

"And then?"

Dylan brought her hand to his lips and kissed it. Then he shot her one of the smiles his mother had once said should be outlawed. "And then, Ms. Singer, how do you feel about attending a charity gala in London?"

* * * *

"Got a call from the State Police in Luzern County. Seems an off-duty capital cop stumbled on a crime scene last Wednesday morning on his way home from work. A lone man trapped in a late-model Buick that had crashed off a mountain road and burst into flames."

Today, Michael Parker was wearing a suit of dun brown—a color which, in Pamela's mind, didn't flatter the man anymore than the green one had. His black-rimmed glasses were firmly in place, the expression on his face focused.

"The VIN plate was missing off the dash but the number was still visible on the frame. The car was reported stolen—the same night you two attended Mama Mia at the opera house—from right here in Philadelphia."

"You think this was the car that nearly hit me?" Pamela asked. Just thinking that she'd now had three brushes with death caused a shiver to race down her spine. When she felt Dylan's touch against her hand, she turned hers over, locked fingers with him.

"And the one that was reported being seen in the vicinity of shots fired," the lieutenant said. "The only question is who the vic in the car is."

"My guess would be some unfortunate man from London named Asher."

Pamela turned to look at Dylan. He'd not mentioned the name before, and at her questioning look, he said, "The man who attacked Pamela in Paris had a known associate who left Heathrow with him en route to Philadelphia, but who never returned."

"Do I assume Scotland Yard is on the case?" Parker asked.

"Yes, but I don't have the name of the inspector assigned to the case. I could have my investigator friend give you a call."

"You do that. In the meantime, we've had no luck locating the missing snitch or any of his friends. That part could take time." He closed the folder on his desk. "We'll work with Scotland Yard to identify the burned remains, have them shipped back if your guess pans out. You're both free to go."

"Thanks, Mike."

Pamela stood with Dylan, appreciating his closeness. Being in the police building, speaking to a cop, made her very uncomfortable.

"Watch your back, Dylan," Parker said as the two men shook hands.

"I intend to."

* * * *

Dylan Pierce shook his head as he watched Pamela quickly flip through the racks of gowns. There was one thing about the lady he knew with absolute certainty.

She could teach stubborn to mules.

His offer to purchase her a gown for this evening's gala event at the Royal Carstairs Hotel was, without doubt, a reasonable one. Her attendance with him tonight was doing him a huge favor.

But of course, the woman wouldn't listen to reason. He could pay for meals. He could pay for entertainment on dates. He could even pay for stays at hotels—and since so far they'd all been *his* hotels, in a way, that was nothing at all. But that was where she drew the line.

The only gift he'd been able to purchase for her had been that bouquet of flowers the night they'd gone to the Academy of Music in Philadelphia.

He pushed away the sense of dread that wanted to surface with that particular memory.

Pamela held up a dress in a deep, shimmering gold. "What do you think?"

Dylan was no fool. His mother had trained him well. "That whatever you want to buy will look stunning on you."

"Careful. I have what my sisters have termed a sick sense of humor. You might regret those words."

Dylan could have told her he might come to regret a lot of things in the next little while, but those words would not be among them. What he said was, "Why don't you try it on?"

Moments later, when she emerged from the dressing room to twirl before him, he forgot all the words of wisdom his mother had shared with regard to keeping his true opinions to himself.

"You look like a flame. A hot, vibrant, compelling flame." And he very much feared he was a moth being drawn inexorably to the fire.

"Then I guess I have a winner."

* * * *

The concert was over, and the guests—a mixture of the well heeled and well known—were down to the mingle-and-be-seen portion of the program.

Dylan had grown up attending charity galas, lavish parties, and star-studded events. As an adult, often these occasions were all part of business, be it his grandmother's or his father's. He'd attended all sorts of soirees with numerous women, and even the most sophisticated of his dates had become at least a little star-struck on occasion.

He sensed none of that from Pamela. She hadn't asked him even once to introduce her to any of the famous personalities in attendance. *The woman becomes more of an enigma the longer I know her.*

"Would you like a drink?" he asked as he placed his hand at the small of her back and guided her out of the crowd.

"Yes, please. How long are you obligated to stay?"

He led her over to one of the bars that had been set up on the edges of the ballroom. Waiters circulated the large area, bearing trays of champagne, but Dylan already knew Pamela didn't care for the beverage. "You're not even a little star-struck, are you?"

"Afraid not. Some of these people achieved fame through the arts, and that's fine. I'm not much of a movie fan, and I've always thought it completely absurd that, as a society, we worship people for those talents rather than their contributions to bettering the human condition. The others are famous only due to accidents of birth."

"You're a very interesting woman."

"Thank you."

"You're welcome. What will you have to drink?" he asked, since the bartender had turned his attention to them.

"Perrier with lime, please."

Dylan asked for a glass of whiskey for himself then turned back to Pamela. "You're not much of a drinker, either, I've noticed."

"Oh, I like the occasional glass of wine, shot of rum, or even bottle of beer. But what I remember of my mother—which isn't much—is the overwhelming smell of mint attempting to mask alcohol. And I've been told my father liked to indulge himself in drink and drugs, too. Their addictions killed them both. So I stay away from the latter and partake sparingly of the former."

Something in what Pamela had just said sparked his curiosity. He turned to receive his order from the bartender.

"My God, they'll let any slut into these events for the price of a ticket."

The scathing female voice came from behind him and to his left. It wasn't until he'd turned around, however, that he realized the remark had been aimed at Pamela.

His woman didn't seem to be particularly insulted by the barb. He thought the other woman must be a friend—as he'd discovered some time ago that female friends often called each other "slut" as a term of endearment. That idea died a very quick death.

"Are you complaining, Mary Ellen, or bragging?" Pamela asked.

"Bitch."

Before Dylan realized her intent, Mary Ellen tossed whatever had been in her glass at Pamela, catching her square in the face.

Then she turned her vitriol on Dylan. "Are you with this tramp? Best watch your wallet—and your will. She fucked my uncle for a few months and then fucked me out of a good chunk of my inheritance. Don't say I didn't warn you."

She turned, head held high, and pushed through the murmuring crowd that had gathered. Dylan's eyes took in the rigid back with just a speck of brown showing right above the low-cut back of her gown.

The bartender had come out from behind the bar and handed Pamela a white linen napkin. An older woman who'd been just behind her had stepped forward and was holding her purse so she could mop up.

"What a dreadful creature," the matron commented to various mumbles of assent from the crowd.

"Are you all right?" Dylan wondered why he asked such an inane question.

"Just peachy. Except now I smell of cheap gin."

"I beg your pardon. Our hotels serve only the most expensive gin."

Pamela's head snapped up at that. Then she laughed, a low, rolling laugh that made him smile. He had to admire her pluck. From the looks on the faces of those closest, her comment and laughter won their approval, too.

She thanked the lady who'd held her purse then turned back to him.

"Can we leave now?"

"I'd say that's a yes." He set down the drink he'd never had the chance to taste. Didn't matter; they'd be in his suite in just a few minutes. He preferred the ambiance there, anyway.

As they left the ballroom en route to the lobby and elevators, Pamela touched his arm lightly.

"Aren't you going to ask who she was?"

"I don't have to. I recognized her." He let that settle. Curiosity furrowed her brow. He'd known the name, of course. Hunter's report had mentioned the McRae family. But that wasn't what he meant. He waited to see if she would ask.

"You do?"

"Yes. She's a spoiled little rich bitch who never worked a day in her life." When Pamela blinked at that, he added, "I recognized the type."

"Oh. Well good, then."

He was done asking her about her past. Too many things simply didn't add up. It was time, he'd decided, to trust his instincts.

As they crossed the lobby, a man lounging in one of the plush armchairs caught his attention. He stopped and waited for Terry Miller to saunter over to them. Not saying a word, Dylan led the way to the executive elevator that was exclusive to the penthouse.

The doors had barely closed when Terry said, "I found out who's put the contract out on your lady."

Chapter 16

"Who in the world is Marcus Danbury? I've never even heard of the man."

Pamela looked from Terry, who'd just imparted the name, to Dylan, who'd immediately cursed and seemed perplexed.

They were in the sitting room of Dylan's suite. Pamela had excused herself just long enough to change out of her gin-soaked dress into a pair jeans and a t-shirt. Dylan had handed her the drink she'd requested downstairs—Perrier and lime—then sat beside her on the sofa.

Terry was looking totally at home in a plush armchair, his own drink in hand. "He fancies himself an entrepreneur, and I suppose, with one semi-legitimate business to his credit, there's some merit to that. But his larger profits come from all sorts of illegal activities, including loan sharking," the investigator explained.

Now Pamela felt perplexed. "Why would such a man want to kill me?"

"He has a moniker," Terry added, "given him by his less genteel associates. They call him The Provider—which means he provides whatever is needed, for a price. Scotland Yard has long suspected that service might extend to arranging contract killings, but they've had no proof."

While Terry's explanation went a long way toward filling in the blanks, it was the expression on Dylan's face that worried her.

"What is it?" she asked him.

"I've never met the man myself. But that one semi-legitimate business Terry mentioned is a casino here in London called the Velvet Slipper."

"I've been there! It was—" she nearly said "with your brother" but changed it at the last minute. "January, I think. I didn't stay long. I'm not a real fan of gambling."

She stopped talking, because the look on Dylan's face told her he knew what she'd meant to say. He caressed her arm.

"It's all right, Pamela. I know that, when in London, Dmitri is a regular visitor there."

It almost seemed he wanted to say more. That maybe, Pamela thought, he was wondering if she'd been targeted to get back at his brother. But he wasn't going to volunteer anything more, and she couldn't, in her heart, hold that against him.

She chose her words carefully. "I broke up with Dmitri that very night—the night he took me there. I can't imagine I've been targeted to get back at him."

Dylan averted his eyes after a moment, which told her he wasn't convinced. She wondered if that was because she wasn't completely convinced, herself. She'd had a feeling from the first that, whatever was happening was tied to Dmitri Andropolis in some way.

"Well, we really won't know anything until I speak to Danbury."

Dylan's announcement made her shiver. "You're going to speak to him?" Pamela didn't think that was necessarily a good idea.

"I'll appeal to the entrepreneur in him." His words might have been casual, but to Pamela, Dylan looked like a man ready to take on the warriors of hell. She pointed a finger at Terry.

"You'll be close by?"

"I'll have our man, here, under surveillance."

It wasn't a lot of reassurance, but Pamela figured she'd take what she could get.

* * * *

"I need to think about getting home." Pamela's words, whispered into the crook of his neck, roused him from semi-sleep.

"You'd trade staying with me and the luxury of the penthouse suite in a five-star London hotel for your flat on the edge of Paris?"

"Trade staying with you? Never. The rest doesn't matter to me. But I have to get back to work, Dylan."

"You need the money?"

"No, I gave my word."

One of the first things he'd personally learned about Pamela was that she did have a passion in life, and that was her work. He'd seen it in her face during the first meeting he'd engineered between them.

"I want to go to the casino this evening, see what Danbury has to say for himself. I'm pretty certain he'll see me without an appointment. Then tomorrow, I'll take you home. I just don't want to leave you alone. One would-be assassin is dead. Doesn't mean there won't be another."

"Dylan...if I'm still in danger, maybe you *should* just let me go home on my own. The closer you stay—well, you're putting yourself in danger, too."

He flipped her over onto her back, looming over her. Taking a moment to tuck some stray strands of hair behind her ears, he let his gaze meet hers and rest there for a moment.

"I don't know what the future holds for us. But I *do* know we have one. Another thing you should know. I'm an old-fashioned kind of guy. This means there is no way in hell I'm going to run away from you just because someone is taking shots at you."

"I see."

Dylan didn't think he'd ever seen quite that look in Pamela's eyes before. He'd spoken only the truth, and he'd moved her. And in turn, felt his heart melt just a little.

Leaning forward, he placed his lips on hers. Intending only a light kiss, he sank fast and deep. He didn't think he'd ever get enough of the flavor of her. Her taste was a part of him now, and his body craved hers, as if it was addicted to her.

Her sweet, needy little whimpers shot his arousal higher, and he levered himself on top of her, aching to take her hard and fast.

The phone rang.

"*Fuck*. Whoever it is can call back."

"But what if it's important?" Pamela stroked his cheek when she asked, which made it hellishly hard for him to think. But she had a point.

"Fuck." He said it a second time, just because he could. Sighing, he rolled off Pamela and picked up the phone on the fourth ring.

"Pierce."

"Dylan."

Just that, his name spoken in exactly that tone by his mother, was enough to send a shiver down his spine.

"Mother. What is it? What's wrong?"

"Dylan...I'm sorry. Dmitri's been arrested."

"*Arrested?* For what?"

"He entered the Golden Fleece after business hours and helped himself to some of the stones in the vault, as well as some of the finished pieces. He was apprehended with the diamonds and rubies, trying to convert them to cash. Dmitri claimed that he was entitled to the merchandise, based on his family connection to the place. Since your grandfather still owns the jewelry store outright, the police contacted him."

"I see." Dylan felt as if all the air had gone out of the room. He'd known, deep down inside, that his brother had problems. He'd known that Dmitri had difficulty with authority, with accepting limits as a teen and young man. But until this moment, it had simply never occurred to him that his brother could really be a criminal.

"Grandfather had him charged." Of course he did. Buried in the recesses of his memory were arguments, chiefly between his grandfather and his brother, about Dmitri's lack of ambition, his lack of industry, and sometimes, his lack of morals.

As a little brother whose hero he was, Dmitri could do no wrong. But Dylan was no longer a little boy. Perhaps the time had come for him to take the blinders off.

"Dylan…this isn't the first time he's taken what wasn't his. And I'm not just talking about the money he took from the company so recently. Your grandfather believes, this time, Dmitri should be held accountable for his actions. And so do I."

His father, Dylan knew, would support his mother in whatever she'd decided to do.

"Where is he?"

"He is being held in custody at the Korydallos prison."

"What about bail?"

"Your grandfather has used his influence with the judge. Release has been deferred until your brother has a psychiatric evaluation. He must agree to this, and so far he has not. Dylan…I must ask you to accept this decision."

His mother rarely asked anything of him. He knew how much she loved both her sons, and he knew she understood what his brother had always meant to him.

"All right." He loved and respected his parents and Grandfather Leandros. They never would have taken these steps unless they believed them to be the right ones. "Yes, I'll honor your decision. But I do want to see him."

"We expected nothing less. I'm sure your brother will be cheered by your visit."

And Dylan knew, in his heart, that his mother had said that for his benefit, that she really believed the exact opposite.

"Your father is sending the jet back for you. It will land in London within the hour."

"Thanks. I'll see you soon, Mother."

He hung up the phone, his thoughts scattered, unable for the moment to think of what came next. He felt the movement on the bed an instant before a sleek feminine arm surrounded his shoulders.

"Dmitri?"

He didn't have to think about whether or not he'd tell her. The words tumbled from him, not just relating the news his mother had delivered, but about his childhood, and the way his brother had always taken care of him, protected him. When he fell silent, she hugged him.

"Of course you have to go."

"I'll have Terry accompany you back home. Please, Pamela—" he sensed she was about to argue, "—I need to know you're safe."

"All right. You'll leave soon?"

"Within the hour." Unlike every other time he could recall, he felt no joy at the prospect of this journey home.

* * * *

Pamela humored Terry, waiting in the car while he unlocked her apartment, checked the premises thoroughly. She knew someone had tried to kill her, but this was *home*. It was practically impossible to accept that there could be any danger to her here.

"That's a top-rate security system you have," he said once they were both inside the building.

"Thanks. It lets my clients sleep easier at night, knowing their art is protected."

"I'll have men posted around the clock, who'll be checking in with me on a regular basis. Please keep the door locked. If you intend to go out, call me. Here's my cell number."

Pamela took the card he proffered, slipping it into her pocket. "I'd feel a lot better if you had someone on Dylan's back, too." She'd made essentially the same argument to Dylan, who'd waved off her concerns.

"I do," A smile split his face, and Pamela realized it was probably the first time she'd seen the man smile. "He just doesn't know about it, of course."

"Good."

Terry left, and Pamela locked the door after him. This flat had been home for more than two years, and she'd always felt not only safe, but complete here. *Until now.* Shaking her head, she understood what was missing—or rather, *who* was missing. Until Dylan returned, she wouldn't feel complete.

Knowing there was only one thing that would settle her nerves and ease her mind, Pamela headed for her studio.

She needed to work, and usually nothing stood in the way of that desire. But being here, looking at the canvas on the easel, her blood didn't race with the same eagerness as it usually did. Part of her wished she'd gone with Dylan.

She had a feeling that this meeting with his brother was going to be very difficult for him.

* * * *

At the sound of the door opening, Dylan spun on his heel. He didn't know what he expected to see, but he was at once relieved and concerned at his brother's appearance.

They'd removed his belt and tie, and his shoes had no laces. But the arrogance Dmitri wore like a second skin was still intact and in place.

"It is about time someone came. I've been forced to remain here since last evening. The judge ordered that no bail is to be set until I submit to a psychiatric examination. This is an outrage! Someone has gotten to the judge, and when I find out who is responsible for this indignity, I will see that person punished."

No time for the niceties. Several times in the past, his brother had been brusque to the point of rudeness, usually during some crisis or other. Dylan imagined that being arrested and having spent the night in prison would qualify as a crisis in anyone's book.

Dylan had never been inside the Korydallos prison before. He knew that in recent times the government had been working to improve conditions at this aging Athenian institution. But he'd never had cause to visit the complex until today. The interview room they were in had one window with bars across it. The sunlight allowed in by this tiny opening seemed weak and watery. The entire scene was like a slice of unreality. The only normal thing was that there was no glass separating them. *That would have been a bit too much to take.*

"Have you not spoken to an attorney?" Dylan had told his mother he'd honor the family's stand on bail; that didn't mean he couldn't ensure his brother's rights were being respected.

"Attorney? You mean the sycophant Mother sent? I fired him, of course. All he could do was mouth platitudes, that no one would know of my being seen by the psychiatrist, that I would be transferred to the psychiatric wing right here in Korydallos, and that I must voluntarily agree to this before bail will be allowed. Bullshit, all of it! I refuse, and they cannot make me. I do not need to see a psychiatrist. I need my freedom and my reputation restored. So, little brother, how have you arranged for me to get out of here?"

Dylan shook his head slowly. "I have no plan to get you out of here, Dmitri."

The change was instantaneous. Dmitri's expression turned scornful. "Then why the fuck did you come? Do you think I want to actually waste time talking to you? Perhaps you want to bend my ear, regale me with tales of your corporate daring-do. Oh, I know, you want to tell me about the banter between you and your father as you shot a round of golf and laughed at my predicament!"

This venom was something Dylan had never experienced before. He'd heard others comment on his brother's disposition, of course. But this was the first time he'd actually witnessed it.

"I came because you're my brother. I love you, and I'm worried for you."

"Well now you can run off and report to Mommy and Daddy that your duty is done. And you and Daddy can open a bottle of champagne and celebrate. I am out of your way. You can become the heir apparent, which is what you've wanted all along. Do not deny it!" Dmitri's face had undergone a transformation as his attack escalated. Such hatred twisted his features that no sign of the handsome, confident man Dylan had always known, remained. "From the moment your father married my mother, this moment has been planned. It was inevitable."

"You're wrong. Father has tried time and again to build a relationship with you. And I thought I had one."

It seemed as if his brother didn't hear him any longer. Dmitri began to pace, left arm folded across his chest, right arm bent at the elbow so that his right hand could stroke the side of his face.

"I know who is really to blame. I know. This is all that bitch's fault. That's when things started to go wrong. When that bitch dumped me. Me! Dmitri Antonio Andropolis. I should have put her in her place from the start instead of trying to act the suave and sophisticated lover. Yes, that's where I went wrong."

Dylan actually felt his blood begin to boil. He took one step closer to Dmitri before asking, "What are you talking about?"

"Yes, it's all her fault. I see where I went wrong with her. If I'd given her a proper beating the first time I had her alone, she wouldn't have caused a scene at Marcus's just because I lost a few hundred thousand pounds. She would have accepted the back of my hand as proper discipline instead of acting the offended *lady* and leaving me. Everything would have worked out if only she had known her place. It's all her fault."

Dylan had his brother by the throat, slamming him against the wall in a heartbeat. Violence surged from every pore, and he wanted, desperately wanted for the first time in his life, to cause serious pain to someone.

"You laid hands on her?" Dylan slammed him against the wall a second time. "You bastard, you *hit* her?"

The two guards raced into the room. It took both of them to pull Dylan off his brother. Dmitri shook himself, and the look that came over him then, Dylan thought, was pure evil.

"What does it matter? She's only a cunt."

In that moment, the bonds of brotherhood shattered. As images from his childhood raced across his mind, Dylan saw his brother's actions in a new light.

Dmitri was no longer the man Dylan had always believed him to be. Maybe, he thought as the guards removed the prisoner from the room, he never had been.

Chapter 17

The banging pulled her out of the zone.

Pamela blinked, feeling somewhat disoriented as she looked around her studio. She'd so successfully lost herself in the art, that coming back to reality was nearly painful. The banging erupted again. Recognizing the sound even as she shook her head at her own quirkiness, she headed toward her front door. Shooting a quick glance at the clock, she saw it was after midnight. Outside, the sound of rain dancing to its own particular rhythm against the slate roof was a welcome, comforting presence. *How many times in my life has the patter of rain lulled me to sleep?*

Approaching the door, she wondered for one instant why Terry or one of his men hadn't called her if she had a *legitimate* visitor. The answer came into view the moment she peered out the security viewer. Drenched and getting wetter, Dylan stood on the stoop.

She disengaged the alarm system and flipped open the locks. Pulling the door open, she stepped back, giving him room to enter.

"Dylan!" She laughed his name, because he kicked the door shut and immediately captured her face between his wet, cold hands.

"I love you."

He caught her gasp of surprise with his mouth, kissing her thoroughly as he backed her toward her bedroom.

"Dylan, what—"

"I don't care about your reputation. Not one whit."

His lips took hers again, and she began to drown in the taste and the heat of him.

"I don't care about your past or about anything at all except you and me and who we are when we're together."

This time when his lips settled on hers, when his tongue plunged, she joyfully wrapped her arms around him and gave in to the need to taste him, to pleasure him, and yes, to soothe him, too.

Stroking his face, she basked in his absorbed attention as he opened buttons, unfastened clasps, and got her out of her clothes. Not saying a word, he stepped back just long enough to whip off his own garments. Pulling her into his arms, he lowered them both to the bed.

"Let me love you." His plea, whispered against her neck as he pulled her closer, sent tiny, flickering shocks along her skin. They were breast to chest, thigh to thigh, with not even a wisp of air between them. His lips found hers again, and as his tongue stroked hers, she sensed such an intense heat she wondered she didn't melt completely. When his mouth moved down her throat, when his lips and tongue and teeth teased the flesh of her nipple, shivers of arousal rushed through her body.

He needed this, she realized as he caressed and kissed and suckled. He needed to lose himself in her. With hands that stroked and a litany of sounds that bore no meaning except to bring comfort, she gathered him in and relinquished herself to his touch.

No sacrifice, this. To be cherished as never before, to be worshipped and loved by a man whose sole focus she was became the sweetest thrill, the most seductive pleasure she'd ever known.

Reaching up, she gave him her mouth and all that she was. When he tore open the foil packet and protected them both, she opened to him eagerly, pulling him down and pulling him in. When he sank into her, she wrapped arms and legs around him, squeezing him with her inner muscles, releasing herself to the moment and his absolute possession.

"I love you, Dylan."

"Pamela!"

Orgasm exploded, fierce and simultaneous, and she gave herself up to the power of the climax and the care of the man inside her.

* * * *

"You should have told me what he'd done to you, sweetheart."

Content and replete now that he'd lost himself in Pamela's body, Dylan stroked her, back to bottom, and let his words settle in the quiet bedroom.

How could he explain the sense of peace he felt right now? Up until she'd opened her door to him, he'd been consumed with a combination of rage and uncertainty. His visit with Dmitri had ripped the underpinning of his life, and nothing had seemed real or solid.

Until Pamela had opened her door, her heart, and her body, and let him in.

Now he felt restored, and he knew this new order that was his reality was a more balanced and a more encompassing one than that just passed. Now he could think and reason and live.

"Would you have believed me?"

Dylan closed his eyes as the veracity of the answer to that question, the pain of it, echoed within him. "No. No more than I believed anyone who would try to tell me that my brother wasn't quite the hero I'd believed him to be."

"But he was, wasn't he? At one time he was a hero to the smaller-than-average, gangly, thirteen-year-old boy adjusting to the reality of life at Eton. And to the fifteen-year-old who raided his father's liquor cabinet."

"I'm not so sure anymore. The man I just left is one consumed by bitterness, convinced we've all been out to get him all these years, when nothing could be further from the truth. I doubt if anything I ever believed about him was ever true."

"Oh, Dylan, no!"

He released her when she moved. Sitting up in the bed, she turned to him. Her expression was so earnest and serious—and in total contrast to her complete nudity. Even though he'd just sated himself in her, he wanted her again. Dylan was beginning to wonder if there would ever come a time when he wouldn't want her.

When she picked up his hand and stroked it gently, he ignored his need and gave her his full attention.

"I'm not saying that the man he is today isn't bitter," she said quietly, "or that he isn't a criminal. But the man he was to that young boy all those years ago? That man was a good big brother and a hero and played an important part in helping that young boy grow into the good man he is today. You *are* a good man, Dylan Pierce, and Dmitri Andropolis had a part in that. Don't let what he is rob you of the treasured memory of what he was."

"You're incredible." She'd refused to tell him exactly what Dmitri had done to her, but when he thought back to those first days, to her skittishness and her bare explanation that a recent relationship had "gone south," he thought it a miracle that she would open herself to any kind of relationship with him at all. But she had, and opened her arms to him so generously he thought she just might be a miracle. He also couldn't help remembering their fight in Philadelphia, when he told her who he was. He vividly recalled her reaction when he'd tried to stop her from leaving. For that one instant, she'd believed he was going to hit her, as his brother had done. Had that moment made her relive the horror of that earlier attack? And yet, after all of that, here she was doing her damndest to comfort *him*.

"You're incredible," he repeated, "and I love you very, very much."

"I love you, too. That sense of destiny you talked about on Penn's Landing? Just before we made love for the first time? I felt it, too, from the very first moment our eyes met in that gallery."

"That wasn't a line, Pamela. I swear it." She deserved more. "Even when I thought I was setting out to plan a trap, I couldn't seem to do anything about my feelings for you. They always seemed to be at odds with what my head was telling me to do. I think that destiny has had a hand in our coming together. I think we're meant to be."

"I think so, too."

Her smile was a little shy, he thought, and in that instant, she looked like a young girl fresh from college. He laced his fingers with hers and brought her hand to his lips.

"I want to get this threat dealt with so we can get on with our lives. Unfortunately, after my visit with Dmitri, I'm convinced that he's somehow a part of the attempts on your life."

"From what you told me of the visit, it doesn't sound to me as if he's conspiring to see me dead—not that he would be very upset if I was. But it didn't sound as if he knew what was happening to me or that you and I are together."

"That doesn't mean he isn't somehow involved or ultimately responsible for what's happening." He'd spent a lot of time thinking as the company jet brought him to Paris. Those words Dmitri had said were damning. It was clear to him, at least, that Dmitri had had an agenda when it came to Pamela. Dylan had no idea what that agenda could have been or why Pamela's decision to leave him had upset his plans. But he very much wanted to find out. After a life of wearing blinders where his brother was concerned, the time had come to open his eyes fully and learn all that he could.

"I have to be honest and tell you that's my sense of things, too," Pamela said. "What do you suggest we do next?"

"I know how important your work is to you. But I think you should come with me, back to London. I think we may be able to uncover at least a few answers with a visit to Marcus Danbury."

"I thought you wanted to visit him alone?"

"I did. I'm ashamed to say the reason for that was I was afraid of what I might find out about Dmitri." He shook his head, feeling like the world's biggest chump. "All things considered, the least I owe you is full disclosure. Plus, I really don't want to let you out of my sight."

Pamela turned her head as if she could see through the wall into her studio and the canvas that rested on the easel there. Then she turned back to face him.

"If you can give me a few hours, I'm almost done with my initial examination. This is the point at which I submit a report to the museum—of what is needed to repair the painting. There's typically a lag of a week or two between my report and their permission to proceed."

"That's a deal. And while you're finishing up, I'll check in with Terry—and the cops back in Philadelphia."

* * * *

Pamela didn't loathe gambling or casinos. She simply wasn't enthralled with them. Even as an orphaned teen lacking many of the "things" a lot of her classmates had, Pamela had never been one to look on games of chance as a path to riches. She'd always believed in working for what she had. That was one of the reasons the two major bequests she'd received in her life had thrown her for a loop. The money was tucked away, working to earn more. Sometimes she used some of it. But mostly, she lived off what she earned.

The Velvet Slipper was housed in a modern building in the heart of London's nightlife, not far from Dylan's hotel. The summer evening was pleasantly warm, the good weather bringing out many tourists and Londoners in search of a good time. Rain had been called for in the forecast, but so far, it had refused to fall.

Pamela exited the car and waited for Dylan, who was speaking to the driver. Turning away, she looked up at the lighted sign and the building itself.

The last time she'd been here had been on a Saturday night in January, which had turned into the worst night of her life. She hadn't told her sisters everything. She hadn't told them that, in those shock-filled moments, sprawled on the sidewalk, the side of her face feeling on fire and Dmitri looming over her with that glazed look in his eyes, she'd feared for her life. She honestly believed that if he'd gone off like that when they'd been alone, he'd have beaten her more severely, maybe even killed her.

Her shudder at that thought was involuntary. She didn't realize that Dylan had caught it or that he understood it, until he stepped up to her.

"I'm sorry. I didn't think. This is where it happened, isn't it?"

Dylan slipped his arm around her. His words, softly spoken, brushed the shell of her ear. She let herself relax into his embrace, absorbing the comfort he offered. His warmth chased away the memory of another's coldness. This was here and now and in every sense another place entirely from that dark night in the past.

She didn't want to think about it, didn't really want to discuss it. But she couldn't completely ignore his question.

"Yes."

"Someday, not now, but someday when this episode of our lives is well behind us, you'll tell me about it. I suspect you haven't really spoken to anyone of what happened that night. You'll need to eventually, sweetheart. And I need for that someone to be me."

The expression in his eyes was steady as she met his gaze.

"Yes, all right. Someday I'll tell you about it."

"Good." When he wrapped his other arm around her, she nestled close just for a moment. Then she kissed his cheek and stepped back. She wanted, even needed, his comfort and support from time to time. But she would stand on her own two feet.

"Now," Dylan said as he took her hand and began to lead her toward the door, "it occurs to me that in your profession, you would have needed to develop a keen observational skill."

"Yes, you're right. So what's the plan? What am I to be looking for?"

"Anyone who recognizes us, who shows surprise at our being together—and here."

"That doesn't sound like a very complicated plan."

"Well, simpler is always better. Besides, I can't think of anything else. My biggest hope is the man behind this façade will tell us what we need to know. Let's see if Marcus Danbury is receiving guests tonight. Maybe he'll be open to making a bargain."

"I'm not sure I like the idea of bargaining with a man who counts assassins and other criminals among his acquaintances."

Dylan laughed softly then leaned forward and kissed her cheek.

"I *know* I don't like it, darling. Which is why you can be certain that Scotland Yard is going to learn everything I do."

"In that case, I hope your observational skills are equally honed."

"Oh, they are. Let's go. The sooner we can get through this, the sooner we can be back and snuggled under the blankets in my bed."

With one final squeeze of her hand, Dylan led her into the lion's den.

Chapter 18

"Do any of your hotels have casinos?"

They'd spent a few moments in the club room, taking in the setup of the lounge, checking out the people sitting at different tables, enjoying drinks and maybe a time-out from gambling. An archway against the far wall led to the gaming room. When they walked under the arch into the casino proper, the sound of slot machines became audible but was muted. Those, Dylan knew, would be in a separate room.

Now he turned his attention from scanning the room to Pamela and her question. "We have a few, yes. It's difficult to own a hotel in some cities and not have a casino. Why do you ask?"

"It just occurred to me that you and I are probably looking at this place from totally different perspectives right now. I'm noticing the ambience of the room, the décor, and the different classes of people here. By the way, we aren't, at the moment, drawing any undue attention from anyone."

"Good." He let his gaze wander around the room until he found what he was looking for. "Ah, there he is." Dylan put a hand at the small of Pamela's back, escorting her toward the corner by the roulette tables.

Pamela looked in the direction that had his attention. "There who is?"

"The manager of this fine establishment."

"You recognize him?"

"No, I recognize the stance."

Judging from appearance alone, the man could have served his employer equally well as a bouncer. Big and burly, hair cropped short, he was dressed in navy blue Brooks Brothers—Dylan recognized the designer's touch, as he owned several of them himself. But aside from the expert tailoring, closer inspection revealed intelligence in the man's eyes and alertness to his bearing. At their approach, he turned his body slightly, and Dylan knew he would be capable of carrying on a conversation with them and keeping his eye on the room at the same time.

"Good evening, Lucas." Dylan had read the man's name tag and title—Manager—which were plainly in sight. "Dylan Pierce and Pamela Singer would like to speak to Marcus Danbury, in private. We'll be over at the roulette tables."

"I'm not certain the gentleman is taking visitors this evening, but your request will be conveyed to him." The voice was softer and more cultured than he'd expected. Dylan smiled, because he knew he'd disconcerted the man.

The average casino visitor didn't know the name of the man who signed the staff's paychecks.

"You just picked the one game I like," Pamela said as they turned their back on Lucas. "Are you sure he was the right one to ask? He doesn't seem to be doing anything about our request."

"He doesn't have to. He's wired for sound. Even as we speak, someone in a back room is relaying our request."

There were four roulette tables in this room. Not surprisingly, the one with the higher minimum bet was the least crowded. Dylan chose a spot midway between the end of the table and the wheel, giving them full access to the game. Reaching into his front jacket pocket, he pulled out his wallet. Tossing a few bills on the table, he turned to look at Pamela's raised eyebrow as the croupier took his money and gave him casino chips in return.

"What?" The expression on her face was too intriguing for him not to ask.

"Do you by any chance own a silver money clip?"

Dylan frowned at the non sequitur. "No, I don't. Why?"

"Just confirming one of my own earlier observations."

In response, he handed her a chip. She placed it on the corner that touched four numbers—seventeen, eighteen, twenty, and twenty-one.

"That only plays eight-to-one," he said, trying to hold back his smile. Before meeting Pamela, he'd have sworn, based on all the information he had, that she'd have played a number, straight-up.

"That means I have four chances in thirty-seven to win. That's better odds than in the States, where the tables have the "double ought" option, too. There I only have four chances in thirty-eight."

"I'm not certain that's how the odds are really calculated. You're not much of a gambler, are you?"

"Well, I don't mind betting on sure things. But beyond that, I find gambling in and of itself is a waste of time and money."

Dylan laughed and put two chips on the number thirteen. "Sweetheart, if it's a sure thing, then it's not *gambling*."

"Exactly!" Her smile told him she was pleased he understood her.

"No more bets, please." The croupier spun the wheel one way and sent the tiny ball spinning on the tilted track above it in the opposite direction. Dylan continued to scan the room around him, even as most of the people—Pamela included—had their attention on that little white ball. He resisted the urge to look until he heard the telltale clatter of the ball dropping onto the wheel.

"Twenty-one, red."

"You won!"

In her smile, he read the thrill of winning the *game*, not the money. He also noted that she'd said "you" and not "I," even though she'd been the one to place the chip on the table. Dylan couldn't resist stroking his finger down her face.

"So we did."

The croupier placed the marker on the number twenty-one, removing all the chips that were on other numbers from the table before beginning to pay out.

"By the way, I thought Terry was going to be with us tonight." Pamela looked up at him, her voice quiet.

"He's outside. Some of his men are inside, so we're covered well enough."

"Until Mr. Danbury decides to see us."

"Well, yes. Until then. Be vigilante, please. I may need you to save me."

He watched as Pamela looked down, her eyes widening as she took in the value of the casino chips the croupier had placed before her.

When she turned to him, her expression horrified, he said, "Well, that *was* a five-hundred-pound chip you played."

"I think I'll let you play the rest, thank you. I'm the kind of person who, when in Vegas, entertains herself for hours at the nickel slots."

"Ladies and gentlemen, place your bets."

Dylan picked up three five-hundred-pound chips and placed them all on the number three. "For you and your sisters," he said.

"Um…are *you* much of a gambler?"

"Not usually when it comes to money."

She met his eyes, and it was as if the busy casino ceased to exist. He saw that she understood his inference, and the level look she gave him in return spoke volumes. She hadn't enlightened him with regard to her past, and that omission was deliberate. This was something he'd suspected, and now having it confirmed, he understood that, somehow, this was how it was meant to be between them.

She'd taken a couple of steps out on the branch of faith herself, first in opening herself to a relationship after the disaster of her association with Dmitri, and secondly by forgiving him his deceit and welcoming him back into her bed.

He had to accept her on faith, too. *Without one word of explanation*. That, he thought, was destiny's bill for the gift of her.

He wasn't going to tell her he'd asked Terry to dig into her past. He'd had a specific reason for doing that, which had nothing to do with obtaining answers about the lady herself. What Terry was looking into had more to do with putting puzzle pieces together.

"No more bets, please."

Dylan noticed as a man who'd come into the room from the back approached Lucas. He turned his attention back to the roulette wheel even as Lucas left his post and came toward them.

"Number three, red."

"You see?" He took Pamela's hand in his and gave it a squeeze. "I bet on a winner."

They were joined by the manager just as the croupier delivered his winnings. "Mr. Pierce, Ms. Singer? Mr. Danbury will see you now. If you'll come with me?"

Dylan pocketed his chips and turned to Pamela. "Shall we?"

"I guess it's show time."

Her words were whispered loud enough for only him to hear. Locating one of Terry's men with his eyes, he gave the man a slight nod. Taking Pamela's hand in his, he followed Lucas.

* * * *

Marcus Danbury was a surprise to her.

Appearing suave and sophisticated, with threads of silver woven through the dark hair at his temple and hands that felt pampered when they shook, he was the kind of man that, in the past, Pamela usually met and befriended. Standing when they entered the room, he offered them first tea, and then stronger drink. She wondered if he was going to try to play some sort of game with them, but his opening words were straight to the point.

"I'm delighted to see you, Ms. Singer."

Well, two can play that game. "You can't be that delighted, Mr. Danbury. The fact that I'm still alive must have cost you a chunk of your money—and a bite out of your reputation."

"Oh, not at all. I'm in the business of seeing to it that suppliers meet consumers, nothing more."

His smile looked almost beatific, but he'd just likened arranging for an assassination to selling produce at the supermarket.

"You're admitting to having had a hand in the attempts made on Pamela's life?"

Dylan's question, so quietly asked, would have sounded like any other conversational gambit. *Unless, of course, you knew him.* Pamela didn't doubt for a moment that, when necessary, Dylan could be a very dangerous man. She wondered if, sitting across from him, Marcus Danbury realized this fact as well.

"Mr. Pierce, you're a businessman. You know the art of the compromise, of the deal, as well as I do. This office is sheathed by electronics, which make any attempt at recording a failure, and all anyone listening in will hear is static. Having said that, there is of course no evidence that I did indeed have any part in the unfortunate events that have so recently taken place in Philadelphia and Paris."

"We never mentioned either of those cities." Pamela had to suppress the urge to smack the smug smile off the man's face.

She didn't know why she'd first thought he appeared sophisticated and urbane. Looking at him now, she could see he was only a thug in designer clothing.

"I read a lot of international newspapers, my dear. I find it useful to keep up on events."

"Let's cut to the chase, shall we? Ms. Singer and I have no interest whatsoever in seeing you suffer any legal consequences for your recent...poor choice in business ventures. All we want is to know who initiated the deal. Who's got an interest in seeing Pamela dead?"

Danbury sat back, taking a moment to have a sip from his glass of cognac. Pamela thought he believed himself to be in possession of all the aces, and in some ways, he was. She really was beginning to feel slimy just being in the man's presence.

"Mr. Pierce." His voice chided as if talking to a recalcitrant child. "You must understand that confidentiality plays a significant role in my…business negotiations. However, you are the brother of one of my best customers. As well, I've always believed that a savvy businessman must recognize when a more lucrative arrangement is in the offing and conduct himself accordingly."

Pamela knew that this is what Dylan had been counting on—that Danbury would want to cut a deal. She turned her attention to Dylan.

If he was aware that Pamela watched him, he gave no sign.

"And you are, of course, a savvy businessman." Dylan's tone, quiet, nearly made Pamela shiver. She hoped he never spoke to her that way.

"As are you. Now, Dmitri, on the other hand, suffers from a shameful lack of self-discipline. He reacts on emotion rather than relying on cool logic. This is an unfortunate trait in him and has been the source of many of his…shall we say…recent problems."

Something in the way Danbury looked at her made her skin crawl. She wondered if he was referring to the incident last January. Even though it had happened out on the sidewalk, she'd be willing to bet Danbury had watched the incident via camera.

"Since my brother is not here to speak in his own defense, I suggest we leave him out of our conversation. Besides, he has no part in these particular…negotiations."

"As you wish, Mr. Pierce. Now, as I see it, you're a gentleman with a need. You need to know who hired a certain late but not lamented young English…freelancer. I'm a gentleman with a need, as well. I have a couple of friends—accountants both—who are in need of good positions with an impeccable company. The Moerae Corporation, under the expert leadership of your father, is one of the fastest growing, most respected companies in all of Europe. I'm certain there's room there for two eager young employees. The

Americans, I believe, have an expression." He turned and offered Pamela a smile before turning his attention back to Dylan. "You scratch my back, and I'll scratch yours."

For a long moment, silence filled the stylish office. Pamela wondered what was going through Dylan's mind. He turned just then and looked at her. In response to his expression, she smiled.

"Mr. Danbury, my back just isn't quite that itchy." He slowly got to his feet. "I'll have to see what I can do to satisfy my curiosity some other way."

"Again, as you wish. Should you change your mind, Mr. Pierce, you know where to find me. Oh, and do give my regards to your brother—as I doubt I'll be seeing him in person anytime soon."

"I'm sorry," Pamela whispered to Dylan as they were escorted back to the gaming floor. "I know you were counting on being able to come to an arrangement with the man."

"Don't apologize, sweetheart. His price was way too high. Does he think I'm some sort of an idiot, to let two people on his payroll into our company?"

"I don't know if that's what he thought, but I do believe he grossly underestimated you."

"Thank you, sweet." They were back in the main casino, and Dylan turned and gave her a light kiss on the lips. "What do you say we cash in these chips and call it a night? Our evening wasn't a complete loss, as I am walking out of here several thousand pounds richer."

Pamela sighed. Leaving sounded like the perfect plan to her. "That's a good idea."

There wasn't much of a lineup at the cashier's cage. Soon, there was just one gentleman ahead of them. He finished his business, turned, and almost plowed into Pamela.

"Oh, I'm terribly sorry—Pierce! Fancy running into you here."

In his thirties, nicely dressed, the man sported a Rolex on his arm, a money clip in his hand, and an expression that shouted guilt. At least to Pamela, it did.

"Abbott. I forgot you were headquartered in London now. Your parents are well?"

"Um, yes," he replied, looking from Dylan to her, his discomfort plain.

Dylan obviously mistook the cause of his discomfort. Pamela nearly smiled. He'd been able to pigeonhole the manager, but she could spot the fish out of water. She kept her smile placid as Dylan performed the introductions. "Pamela, this is a friend of my brother's. Peter Abbott, Ms. Pamela Singer."

"Pleased to meet you."

His eyes had widened for one fraction of a second, filled with recognition. His response was proper and phony as hell.

"Mr. Abbott."

There was a brief silence, then Peter looked over Dylan's shoulder. "Well, you'll have to excuse me. I must be off. Lovely seeing you. My best to your parents."

Before either of them could say a word, he nodded politely and headed for the door.

"I'll just be a moment," Dylan said. While he stepped forward to exchange his tokens, Pamela kept her eyes on Abbott. The man looked over his shoulder just once as he reached the door. Fear lined his features, and Pamela felt a compelling urge to follow him as he absolutely fled.

"What is it?"

Dylan had finally noticed her frown. He'd put his arm around her and began to slowly walk with her toward the exit.

"You said to let you know if anyone recognized us? That man just did."

A look of dawning realization lit Dylan's face. "Well, son of a bitch, so he did. Let's go."

"We may already have lost him," she said as they began to jog toward the door. "He practically ran out of here."

"Doesn't matter," Dylan said, anger lacing his voice. "I know where the prick lives."

Chapter 19

When Dylan exited the Velvet Slipper, Pamela close on his heels, Terry Miller was waiting for them.

While they'd been inside, clouds had rolled in, and a fine drizzle drenched the air and the ground. The mist could easily morph into a fog, Dylan thought, as Terry drove them through the wet streets of London. The pavement, still warm from the sun, turned the light rain to steam.

"He looked like an assassin was after him when he bolted out the door. Thought something might be up, there, so I had one of my men follow him."

"Thanks for that." Dylan offered Pam the front seat, but she elected to sit in the back instead. "He certainly didn't seem to be too happy to see us."

Terry's cell phone rang, and he answered it while steering the car through traffic. "No, just stay put," he said to the caller. "We're on our way." When he ended the call, he said to Dylan, "He didn't go home. He's over at a pub on Queen Victoria Street. Black Friar's."

"You know, in all that activity back at the casino, we never took time out for a nice pint of beer." Pamela's observation made Dylan smile.

"You're right, we didn't." To Terry he said, "I wonder why he picked a known tourist attraction to run to."

"Could be he's meeting someone there. Makes sense, really. Hiding in plain sight, if you will. Not to discount the fact that it's a safe place to 'bump into someone' you might not otherwise have a good excuse for meeting."

"You know," Pamela said quietly, "he was unnerved as soon as he saw you, Dylan. Before he even knew who I was."

"I noticed that. And I did notice his reaction to hearing your name."

"It could be as innocent as your brother trash-talking me to him."

"Sweetheart." He turned in his seat so he could look at her. "Thank you. But we both know there's nothing innocent about Dmitri or this entire situation."

Terry maneuvered the car into a parking spot. He pointed out the windshield. Up ahead, the strange little wedge-shaped building was hard to miss. Dylan fondly remembered his first visit to the establishment. His father had taken him there for his eighteenth birthday and his first legal pint of beer in a pub.

"Busy place."

"It is," Terry answered Pamela's observation. "Some nights it's standing room only."

"If your people are watching the outside, why don't we go in and have a pint…or something?" Dylan suggested.

"Good idea. You and Pamela head in there first. I'll come in a minute or so after. Abbott saw the two of you together, but he hasn't seen me yet. If he tries to give you the slip, I'll nab him."

Dylan thought that sounded like a plan.

* * * *

"It's a royal fuck up, that's what it is."

Peter thought Timmy's assessment was spot on.

"You say the man bought your story, though?" the little cockney asked.

It took effort for him to bring his focus back to the meeting earlier that evening with Danbury. Seeing the Singer woman with Pierce had shaken him badly. "He acted blasé, with a 'thanks for bringing this to my attention' smile and a very offhand manner. But his eyes, his eyes told the tale. They went cold and hard. And there was no surprise in them, either. Like he knows our friend Jeremy and figures this is just something he'd do." Peter looked about, but he and Timmy were crowded around a small table; with so many others in the small room, no one paid them any particular mind. Timmy's idea to meet here had been a capital one. In the midst of a busy pub, lost in a crowd that was drinking beer and chatting, no one even noticed them. Perfect. And since he'd left the casino well ahead of Pierce and the Singer woman, and they couldn't possibly have followed him, he and Timmy were safe for the moment.

"So you think that'll be enough to get rid of Jer? The man will do the deed?"

"Yes, I do. And I don't feel one bloody speck of guilt on the matter, either. Irons would slit both our throats without so much as a moment's thought."

"'e would at that. Any clue if Danbury took the bait about our unknown player?"

Peter picked up his pint, took a long drink. "Hard to tell. A man as well connected as he is has to have a clue who the blighter is. Whether or not he can—or will—do anything about him is anybody's guess. I'll tell you one thing that gave me pause. It occurred to me as I was sitting there in that bastard's proper-looking office that he could be 'The Banker' himself."

Timmy paled at that revelation. "Well, shit. We didn't think of that one, did we?"

"No, we didn't. That thought had barely settled when I ran into Pierce and the Singer woman."

"Fuck. We take one bloody step forward and get knocked two back. What the bloody hell are they doing together, and what in God's name are we going to do now?"

Peter shook his head. He couldn't think of a next step.

He froze when a hand landed hard on his shoulder. Turning his head to the side and up, he met the icy stare of Dylan Pierce.

"Gentlemen, it's so noisy and crowded in here tonight. Why don't we take this party to my place?"

* * * *

Pamela would have laughed at the men's expressions if the situation wasn't so serious. Two more down-trodden and morose faces she'd never seen. As soon as they'd all entered Dylan's suite, he'd headed for the bar. She couldn't blame him. It had been a hell of a night, so far, and was looking to get even worse. They'd not bothered with a pint at the pub. The cathedral-like interior of the historic hostelry, as beautiful as it had been, had been packed nearly to the rafters.

Terry had seated their guests in the sitting room and remained, arms across his chest, standing over them. The guests, in turn, seemed entranced either with their shoes or the carpet.

"Here, love."

Dylan handed her a glass of wine. And he noted, with her, the sharp look from the two men at his endearment to her.

"We'd like some answers, please." She sat on the sofa across from Peter Abbott and the other man, who Terry had announced—after frisking him—as Timothy Sykes.

"'ere now, you know what's going on better than we do."

Sykes's assertion gave her an uneasy feeling. Shaking her head, she looked at Dylan. "I don't, you know."

"Yes, I know." He sat forward, making eye contact with Sykes. "Gentlemen, we're about out of patience."

"Look, Pierce, I don't know what you want. If it's a piece of the action, you'll have to talk to your brother about it. Timmy and I have decided to get out."

"Get out of what?"

Pamela saw the truth in their eyes when they looked at her. They believed she knew whatever secrets they held. More, they seemed almost afraid of her.

For a long moment, no one said anything. Then Abbott turned to Sykes. "If she truly doesn't know any of this, and if he's as straight a shooter as Dmitri always sneered at him for being, they might be able to help us with our exit strategy."

"Are you willing to take that chance, mate?"

"I don't think we have a choice. Do you?"

"Go on, then."

Abbott turned to Dylan. "We have a problem. We want your word that you'll do everything you can to help us out. To give us protection, if you will."

Pamela looked at Dylan as he sat back and took her hand in his. "If you'll accept my word, you have it."

Abbott nodded once. "All right, then. A bit of something to drink first would be much appreciated."

Pamela could see Dylan's patience fairly thinning, but he got up and poured refreshments for the two men. Terry obviously believed the flight danger was over, for he got his own drink then sat down in the remaining chair.

Abbott took one long gulp from his glass then set it down and looked Dylan squarely in the eye. "We're all in a hell of a mess, and Dmitri is at the heart of it."

* * * *

"I don't understand what any of this has to do with Pamela." In the last twenty minutes, Dylan had his worst fears confirmed. Dmitri's transgressions against the family were the least of his sins. For years, his brother had committed felonious acts. He swallowed hard as he wondered how in hell he was going to tell his mother about all of this. The men had paused in their tale, and it was only then he realized that the whole time they'd been speaking, Pamela had been stroking the back of his hand.

Peter Abbott exhaled, sat back, and looked at Pamela.

"About ten months ago, Dmitri came to the group with one of what he and The Banker liked to call their 'business propositions' but which were, in fact, cons or outright crimes."

At this point, Abbott lowered his eyes. Dylan worked to hold back his contempt, but if a trace of it showed on his face, that was fine. These men, along with three others—including his brother—had broken the law, stolen from people. And they'd somehow embroiled his woman in their intrigue. "Go on."

"Dmitri had heard about a woman through someone in his circle, a woman rumored to have a shady past and dubious present. One who, as a hobby, restored paintings—often near-priceless paintings—for museums. Dmitri said he'd done some investigating and discovered that this woman worked from a studio that was in her home on the outskirts of Paris. And he had a plan, he said, that would ultimately net us thousands."

"My God, he was planning to steal from me." Pamela's words sounded hollow. Dylan gave her hand a squeeze.

"In a nutshell, yes. Irons would produce a forgery of whatever piece you were working on. The Banker had buyers lined up— collectors who didn't care if the masterpieces they received were stolen or not. He was even going to reach out through his 'legitimate' channels and arrange for some of the more prestigious galleries to invite you to consult for them."

Pamela turned to Dylan, her look stricken. "I'd had an inquiry from the Imperial Prescott gallery in London just before Christmas. I was so excited, because it would have been the first premier European gallery to give me a chance."

Dylan could do nothing but rub her arm to console her. Seeing that look on her face and the devastation in her eyes obliterated the last of his filial loyalty where Dmitri Andropolis was concerned. He would gladly see his brother roast in hell for what he'd done to this woman.

He turned his attention back to Abbott. "How were they planning to make the switch without it being detected?"

"When the painting was on its way back to the gallery would be my bet," Pamela answered. "They would only have to have an in with someone with the transport company. The final approval of the work is done in my studio, usually by an art expert from the insurance company and an officer from the gallery, and then it's crated by them and shipped. It wouldn't be checked so thoroughly after that."

"And if a substitution was discovered, then Ms. Singer—with her dubious reputation—would be blamed. It was, as Dmitri pointed out, almost the perfect crime. And if the first one wasn't discovered, then a second or a third could follow."

"And I ruined everything when I dumped Dmitri."

"Aye, that was a development no one anticipated. Irons and The Banker were furious with Andropolis. Our unknown partner ordered him to make up with you, but I guess you were having none of him."

"No."

"So what happened after that?" Dylan had a feeling he knew what had happened next, but he needed to have his suspicions confirmed.

"Well, Irons went to see Dmitri, and I guess he got rough with him. Told your brother he owed the group a half a million dollars for the 'shortfall in profits' he'd caused. It was as he was being 'persuaded' that Dmitri told Irons that Ms. Singer here knew the entire plan and the identity of every one of us, *including* The Banker. So there was a meeting in Paris, which we now realize The Banker and Irons orchestrated for more than one reason. They've likely come to terms, the two of them, with the first items on their agenda: getting rid of the rest of us. The Banker arranged the contract on Ms. Singer's life. I was to be the point man there, the one who would check in with Danbury, and I'm ashamed to say I did as I was told."

"It was then we both knew we'd had enough," Sykes chimed in. "We'd never had a hand in violence before. And it only stood to reason that, after Ms. Singer was gone, Dmitri would be next. If The Banker could order the death of one person, he could do another, as well, and we didn't like our chances."

"He's your brother," Abbott concluded. "You can likely get him to tell you who The Banker is. He's the only one who knows his identity. Then you can put an end to this entire debacle. We'll both offer our testimony in court, if that's what it will take. Like I said, we just want to get the hell out of this mess."

Dylan looked over at Terry. "Can you call your contact at Scotland Yard? See what kind of a deal can be made for our boys here?"

"If this Banker can be tied to the murder of Eric Llewellyn in Philadelphia, I'd say the Yard would be happy to deal and serve the American police their killer on a platter."

"Here now, we didn't know about no murder in America!" Sykes's eyes had gone wide, his expression horrified. Looking at Abbott, whose complexion had just paled, convinced him that neither man had known about that. It didn't make up for what they'd both done over the years, but it did, in Dylan's mind, separate them from their partners in crime.

Dylan was certain, from what he'd just heard, that not only was this Banker—whoever he was—responsible for Eric's death, but that he'd likely enlisted the other member of the group as the actual killer.

"Until then, you can see these men are in a safe place?"

"I can."

"And us? What do we do next?"

He met Pamela's steady gaze. "I think I need to have another talk with Dmitri."

"So you're going back to Athens."

He heard the tone of disappointment in her voice and couldn't hold back his smile. He wondered if she found the idea of their being apart as distasteful as he did.

"No, sweet. *We're* going to Athens. After I deal with Dmitri, I'll introduce you to your future mother-in-law."

Chapter 20

Pamela still wasn't certain if Dylan had proposed to her or not.

As the limousine whisked them from the airport to the Carstairs Athens Hotel, she divided her attention between Dylan, who'd fallen quiet, and the scenery that was passing by the window. Funny, but she'd never had that sense of déjà vu that some people talked about. Until now, and this drive through one of civilization's oldest cities.

Something caught her attention, and she turned to see if she could get a better look at it.

"That's the National Monument of Reconciliation," Dylan said.

"Reconciliation for what?"

"Ah…civil war, nineteen forty-five to forty-nine. Is this your first visit to Athens?"

"It is. I'm ashamed to say it's one of the few major artistic centers I've never been to." Since Dylan was being loquacious, she asked, "Are you upset that your mother had a car waiting for us at the airport? Or that the driver told you she was expecting us for dinner?"

Dylan chuckled. "No, I told you that I'd take you to meet her after…well, after."

Pamela leaned across the back seat and placed a kiss on his lips. "I'm sorry. I'm really sorry for everything you learned yesterday about Dmitri."

"I'm the one who should be apologizing to you. Between my brother and I, we've made your life a living hell."

"No."

A glimmer of the man he was had always been right there before her. But it took *this* moment to finally show her that his nobility of character went straight to the bone. Presented with the choice—his brother or her—he'd chosen to believe in her, without a word of explanation or a wisp of proof.

"Dylan, I won't lie to you and say that what Dmitri has done to me, both physically and with his scheming, doesn't matter, because it does. But you sought me out with pure motives, and I realize that. Even when things were at their worst between us, I understood that. I doubt two men in a hundred would go to the lengths you did out of love for his brother. Sitting here, right now, I can tell you that I wouldn't trade a moment of my time with you for anything. Even those days when we were apart and I was licking my wounds, helped to bring us to here and now. I love you, Dylan Pierce, very, very much."

His smile was slow and beautiful, whisking away the shadows she'd noticed in his eyes since the revelations in London.

"Do you love me enough to marry me?"

"But what about all those unanswered questions you have about me?"

"I know everything I need to know about you, Pamela Singer. Whatever was in the past simply doesn't matter. I love you, and I want to marry you."

Deep inside her, down where her soul twined with her heart, a sense of elation, of overwhelming joy and freedom, began to blossom. Pamela had never felt anything like it in her entire life, but she thought, in those first few moments, as Dylan's fervent declaration echoed within the confines of the car, that this was the moment she'd been waiting all her life to live; *this* was the reason she'd been born. The sensation lasted but a heartbeat of time, a heartbeat during which the image of a glistening cavern shimmered in her mind. Within this almost magical space arose a pedestal upon which three women, dressed in white, stood. She felt the presence of her sisters beside her, felt connected to them, as they faced the other three.

Pamela blinked and the image vanished. But the sense of joy remained. Sliding closer to Dylan on the seat, she twined her arms around his neck. "Yes," she said against his mouth. "I want very much to be your wife."

Arms and mouth, heart and soul, she opened to him. This kiss was different from any other. Carnally hot, emotionally poignant, his flavor seeped into her, drenching her completely. The feel of his arms enclosing her, of his tongue stroking hers, aroused her instantly and nearly beyond bearing.

"Hold that thought," he whispered against her lips.

She opened her eyes and stared into his laughing face. Why he was so amused registered a split second later when the car door beside him was opened from the outside.

"I hadn't even realized the car had stopped."

"That, my love, is the nicest thing anyone has ever said to me."

The air was hot and humid. Pamela looked around at the beautifully kept property then up at the rising glass-and-marble structure of the hotel.

"Somehow, I was envisioning something a little more…Grecian in architecture. You know, using white marble and Doric columns. Since we *are* in Athens."

Dylan's laugh was quiet but light, telling her more than words that his heart had been lifted from its previous funk.

"My mother is going to *love* you."

* * * *

It was good to be home. Dylan kept one of the penthouse suites here as his home base. He traveled so much for both his father's and his grandmother's companies, that he'd put off buying a home of his own. He had this suite and one in the San Francisco hotel. But he thought that, since he'd just become an engaged man, he should think about something more permanent. His memory tossed up a recent property he'd seen for sale.

"There's this island in the Dominican Republic." He pulled Pamela close to him as the private elevator sped them up to the top floor of the hotel.

"Yes? You're thinking it would be a good spot to honeymoon?"

"No, actually, I was thinking it would be a good place to live. Part-time, anyway. There's a very nice house on it, with lots of privacy. I was thinking I might buy it."

"You would buy an entire island?"

"Well." He wondered he didn't burst with this happiness that filled him. He could see his future in that moment, and it was a future that included spoiling his woman. "It's a fairly small island."

"A *small* island. Oh, well, that's fine then."

Her dry rejoinder sparked his laughter, lifting the remainder of the pall that had fallen over him since learning the truth about his brother. The elevator doors opened, and he wasted little time getting them into the suite. The door barely closed when he pulled her into his arms.

"Now, where were we?" He gave her no time to answer, surrounding her with his arms and his body, settling his mouth on hers. As his tongue delved and danced, as her flavor became his, he knew that, already, she sustained him. He could go anywhere, do anything, as long as she was a part of him. "Let me have you." He didn't care if his words sounded desperate or not. He needed to be inside her, to connect with her so completely that they truly became one.

"I'm yours."

She understood. Scooping her into his arms, he carried her across the room and up the small flight of stairs to the bedroom. Setting her on her feet, he reached for the buttons of her blouse even as she began to open his. They stripped each other with short, jerky motions. Then he laid her on the bed, loomed over her.

"Will you let me be naked inside you?"

"If you want to make me pregnant, I'll have to go off the pill." She reached up, stroked his face. "But for now, yes, I want you naked inside me. It'll be a first. You'll be the first."

"And the last."

"Yes. And the last."

Dylan kissed her again, his lips and tongue taking and giving as he plunged hard and fast and deep. When her body wrapped around him, when her slick, velvet heat surrounded him, he knew he would never be alone again, that he had finally, truly come home.

* * * *

Pamela knew Dylan hoped Dmitri's acceptance of the release conditions meant he'd taken the first vital step forward. Not for the world would she discourage him in this belief, even though she herself was far from convinced.

A shiver wracked her, and she used her hands to chafe her arms. An uneasy feeling welled in the bit of her stomach. She doubted Dmitri would be as willing as Dylan hoped to reveal the name of the man who had arranged for her death.

The sound of a knock on the door pulled her away from the window and her introspection.

She could see characteristics of both her sons in Maria Andropolis Pierce. Matching her in height, Dylan's mother was lovely—she could have passed for forty instead of the sixty-something she had to be—and her deep chocolate eyes danced with the light of amusement.

"Hello. You are Pamela. My son will be annoyed with me. But it will not last long. May I come in?"

Pamela stepped back, meeting the older woman's smile with one of her own. "No, Dylan isn't one to hold onto grudges, thank goodness."

"Men can be unreasonable at times, don't you think? They can also complicate situations by overanalyzing them. It remains for us women to handle certain details efficiently and with little fuss."

Pamela found she agreed with the woman and then held still as she was scrutinized rather thoroughly.

"Mr. Miller said you were very pretty."

"When Terry told me he had a man watching over Dylan, I wondered if that had been your touch. Thank you, Mrs. Pierce."

"Maria." She waved off the more formal name. Walking over to the picture widows, she looked down at the city below. "A mother always knows," she said quietly.

She looked over her shoulder at Pamela. Sensing an invitation, Pamela walked over until she was standing next to Maria.

"I tried so hard with Dmitri. But nothing I did ever seemed to reach him. He was such a solemn and serious little boy. Very self-contained. When Justin and I married, I hoped a man's influence would be just the thing. My heart broke for the both of them. For Justin, who reached out time and again, only to be rebuffed, and for my son, who for whatever reason could not or would not respond. Because a part of me always knew he would choose the wrong path. This is a failure I will live with for the rest of my life."

"It's not your fault, Maria."

"That's what Justin says. When you become a mother, perhaps you will understand. When the doubts and fears began to whisper in the back of my mind, I should have seen to it that he had professional help. But I lived in denial for too long. I am sorry for all that he has done to you. And I'm very grateful for it at the same time, for Dmitri's scheming brought you into Dylan's life."

Pamela shook her head. "Thank you for that. But the path Dmitri is on is one he chose of his own free will. Let me tell you how I know this to be the truth. I barely remember my own mother. I never knew my father, never even knew his name until—well, until much later in life, and that was pure chance. I was dumped into the system at the age of three, the illegitimate child of an overdosed junkie. I was eleven before I landed in a decent foster home with caring people. That's where I found my sisters. Some people might think that it wouldn't be surprising with that background if I'd turned out bad. But we make our own choices in this life, regardless of how much—or how little—we've been given as children. A part of how each of us turns out does have to do with what's inside us when we're born. But the bigger part, I think, is choice. Dmitri could have chosen to respond to your husband, to accept the hand and the heart being offered. And really, he still could."

"Justin is going to love you."

Pamela actually felt herself blush. Maria laughed, and then her mood turned somber.

"Dylan is going to be disappointed again, I think. And I would not wish sadness or heartache upon him. But he is beginning to see his brother for the man he truly is. This is something that needed to happen, but I am sorry for it, too."

"I know. I think the only thing we can do is just be here for him."

* * * *

"I am shocked, quite frankly, that you would even bother to come here."

Dylan was surprised—not just by his brother's undisguised hostility but by the fact that he had his lawyer present.

He had hoped Dmitri's acceptance of the release restrictions meant he'd chosen to get help and that he was penitent and wanted to make a new beginning. The last of his hope dissipated, and strangely, with it, a weight he'd not even been aware of carrying.

"Do you know why I'm here?"

"Not only do I *not* know, I really don't care."

Dylan simply lost it. For the second time in as many meetings, he hauled his smirking, condescending half brother up by the shirt front.

Only this time, he didn't slam him against the wall, he fisted his right hand and laid a haymaker on him.

"This is assault!" The lawyer jumped to his feet, took two steps toward Dylan, then froze.

No doubt he doesn't like the look on my face. "It's going to be a whole hell of a lot more than fucking assault if I don't get some answers."

"Go to hell."

"No, Dmitri, *you* go to hell. Bad enough you involved an innocent woman in your criminal activities, but you served her up on a platter, offered her as a target—"

"Wolf bait. That is the proper term for your lovely Ms. Singer. I know you've been fucking her, know you've ushered her back and forth across the ocean like a cherished mistress. But she is only a woman and a slut at that. Why would I care what happens to her? Besides, little brother, I'm banking on your ability to keep the slut safe. In so doing, you'll be protecting me."

"You bastard. You fucking bastard. I want the name of the man you're so afraid of!"

Those words had an effect. Dmitri got up off the floor, took a moment to dab at his lip and straighten his clothes. He shot a hostile look at the lawyer. "Leave us."

The lawyer objected immediately. "I do not suggest you be alone with this man, Mr. Andropolis. He has already proven—"

"To be more of a man than I believed him to be. Get out!"

Dylan paced over to the other side of the room. He had to tamp down the urge to beat the living hell out of his brother. If there was even a small chance that Dmitri could be convinced to tell him who had initiated the contract against Pamela, he had to take that chance.

"Would you care for a drink? I could use one myself."

"No. Thank you."

Dylan watched as Dmitri poured himself a scotch on the rocks, his usual. Then as if this were any other visit, lounged lazily in a chair.

"You have to know, there is no way in hell I'll divulge the name of my…what did you call him? Oh yes, *the man I am afraid of.* If that means I have to sacrifice a woman to be safe, so be it. If you're going to lose your head over a piece of ass, that is your problem. Oh yes, I know that you've been enjoying the lovely Ms. Singer for several weeks now—following her over to Philadelphia then Paris, taking her to London. Hell, you even took her to Marcus's casino. You never were able to treat women as the convenient commodities they were meant to be. But that is what you have to do, especially with this little tramp. She's not as innocent as you think. Dylan, my little brother, it is way past time for you to grow up."

He wondered in that moment if his brother realized that, through his posturing, he'd given Dylan the information he'd come for.

"You're right, of course. It is time for me to grow up…to let go of childish things." Slowly, he walked toward the door of his brother's apartment. Without turning back, he said, "Funny thing, perceptions. Given a choice between putting my trust in you or in Pamela, I'd choose her. I have, in fact. We're getting married."

"You'll be sorry!"

"I am already. I'm sorry for a lot of things, both past and present. But not about my decision to marry Pamela."

He let the door to his brother's apartment close behind him. A sense of dread filled him. The need to see Pamela, to have her in his arms, flooded him.

Not questioning the instinct, he ran for his car.

Chapter 21

"Ms. Singer! Ms. Singer! There's been a terrible accident. Mr. Pierce has been taken to the hospital. I've been sent to bring you to him."

The loud pounding on the door and the shouted message froze Pamela's heart for one horrible moment. Racing across the room, she threw open the door.

And came face-to -ace with a man holding a gun.

"Step back please, my dear."

Pamela didn't know this man, had never laid eyes on him before. White hair, fit of form, he wore a three-piece suit with as much comfort as he held the gun. She stepped back. He came forward and closed the door behind him.

"My only regret is that I don't have time to sample you. First Dmitri, and now Dylan. Of course, you've spent your lifetime honing your sexual skills."

"Who the hell are you?"

"Come, come, you know very well who I am. If you require a formal introduction, my name is Hunter Symington. I'm a vice president of the Moerae Corporation. I'm also involved in Dmitri's shall we say…less than noble endeavors. "

"I've never even heard of you."

"Ah, such a good little actress. But then, I would expect nothing less. I can see how you earned the name *The Seductress*. I've heard quite a number of tales about you, my dear."

"Have you?" How long would it be before Dylan came back? Pamela tried to think of some way to gain the upper hand. She'd fought back against that bastard in the alley, and he'd had a knife. But the man facing her with that nasty-looking black gun didn't appear to lack any self-assurance or self-control.

"Yes, indeed. Neil McRae was only too willing to tell me all about the way you'd lured his uncle into your bed and connived your way into his will."

"You know, you shouldn't believe everything you hear."

"Oh, please. Protestations of innocence? Don't waste your breath, my dear. I quite admire your accomplishments, actually. Congratulations on snagging the youngest Pierce. Although I would have thought you'd have been angling for the father. My friend Justin puts on the airs of being faithful to his wife—but he's a man, like the rest of us, and susceptible, like the rest of us, to temptations. I knew, you see, when Dylan stopped contacting me for information, that he was hiding something. It didn't take me long to discover he was the latest to fall under your spell. Amazing how eager some young bucks are to report goings-on if they think advancement is in their future. I took steps, of course. My friend Jeremy helped me with that. Popped over to the States with no problem at all, since he is himself American. Dylan had to be punished for being so weak."

"You had Eric Llewellyn murdered?"

"Yes, and you were to have been charged with it. That didn't work out any better than having Danbury arrange for your demise. So I've decided to take matters into my own hands."

"You're going to kill me? How do you expect to pull that off?" She didn't know if keeping him talking was the best option or not. Because it had suddenly occurred to her that if Dylan *did* come through that door, he would be in grave danger. She couldn't have that.

"Oh, it's really very simple. You and I are going to take a little drive. There's a spectacular view from the cliffs that I insist you see firsthand. While you're feeding the fish, I'll confess to Dylan that you turned your charms on me, and I couldn't resist. That we drove to a secluded spot—I've already paid a witness, by the way—and that you asked me to drop you off at the airport afterward, and I did. I'll even describe the other man who met you there. No one will really be surprised that you played to type and left him for another wealthy, older man."

"Why? Why are you doing this?"

"I'm killing you to protect myself, of course. I can't have you telling my friend Justin about my extracurricular activities. Especially when everything is finally going my way. This is something that has been in the planning ever since Maria Andropolis turned her eyes away from me and on Justin Pierce. She never even saw me after I made the mistake of introducing the two of them. I was far better suited to be her husband, to run her father's businesses. When she married Justin, I knew that, eventually, I'd have to pay them both back.

"Now Dmitri is in disgrace, and I couldn't be happier. I've had to work my entire life to get to where I am, and that little bastard got everything handed to him for nothing. When I found out about his cons, I couldn't *believe* my luck. Here was a way to not only line my pockets but to get Dmitri where I wanted him—at my mercy. His own ego is bringing him down. He's finished. Dylan will be next. Although I don't really have to look for any real weaknesses in him. No, him I will have to kill. Then the way will be clear for me to become even more important to Justin and the company. And when *he* dies—who could blame a man for taking his own life after the death of his only son?—then I'll be there, to take over the company and comfort the grieving wife and mother."

"You're insane! That will *never* happen."

"No, my dear. I'm not insane, simply motivated. Now, if you please, we'll be leaving. As we walk through the lobby, keep in mind that I have a gun pointed at your back. The slightest wrong step and I'll kill you."

"Then you'll get caught." Pamela knew she really had no choice. Once in the lobby, she'd take her first opportunity.

"I might get caught, but with a good lawyer and enough money, I'll probably get off. You, on the other hand, will most certainly be dead."

* * * *

"You!"

Dylan spun on his heel at the sound of the female voice. The woman striding toward him across the marble expanse of the hotel lobby, anger lacing every step, was a stranger to him. Her long red hair streamed behind her as she walked, and he could do nothing but wait as she approached.

"You son of a bitch! Between you and your brother, you've really done a number on her, haven't you? I was going to put you on a pedestal for saving her life in Paris, but that can wait. Because here you are, and where is she? You'd damn well better have someone protecting her, because I can tell you one thing that is fact. Anything happens to my sister and I'll kill you. Or Alba will."

Dylan was feeling much more at ease than he had been. Once in the car, he'd contacted the police, who were even now on their way to question the man Dylan suspected of being the final member of Dmitri's gang. The feeling of dread that had filled him immediately left with that call. He gave the woman before him a big smile. "You must be Twyla. Welcome to Greece. Did you call ahead, book a room? No matter, you can stay upstairs with us. The suite has an extra bedroom." He thought his pleasant manner would poke a hole in her steam, but she didn't even blink.

"Where's P.J.?"

"P.J. Is that what you call her? I prefer Pamela, myself. And she's safe. She's in my apartment here. This hotel is very safe and secure. Even the elevator to the penthouse floor is restricted." As he pointed to the private elevator, he noticed more than a few eyes were looking their way. Placing his hand on Twyla's arm, he pulled her out of the traffic flow. "Did you rent a car at the airport? If you give me your keys, I'll have someone bring in your suitcase. Then I'll take you up, and you can see for yourself that your sister—"

"Your penthouse elevator is coming down."

Dylan turned to look at it. Amusement fled. "She told me she'd stay put until I returned. She wouldn't break her word."

"No, she wouldn't." Twyla didn't send him so much as a backwards glance as she moved away from him, to a point that would put her on the other side of the lobby.

The doors opened, and Pamela emerged. Hunter followed close behind her, and everything inside Dylan went cold. He could see it all on her face. She'd spotted him, but he didn't think Hunter had—not yet. Pamela was no delicate flower, but that didn't mean he wasn't scared witless for her.

Dylan began to move slowly along the edge of the massive space, simultaneously working his way toward the elevator and closer to the pair, hoping to get past them so he would be behind Hunter. Inching along, he didn't take his eyes off the man—or the way he had his hand in his right jacket pocket, and the bulge he could see there.

Movement ahead distracted him. He spotted his mother and fought every urge within him to yell at her to get back. Then he noticed she wasn't looking at him but had her eyes also trained on Hunter and Pamela. He watched, horrified, as she reached out and grabbed up one of the decorative vases on display.

"Hunter! Over here!" His mother's shout coincided with the smash of the porcelain on the marble floor. Hunter's attention was pulled to the left, and Dylan made his move.

He sprang for the older man, wrapping his arms around him and pulling him to the floor at the same instant Twyla leapt forward and yanked Pamela away from him.

Hunter struggled, flailing wildly. Dylan's grasp on him slipped. Symington raised his right hand, gun wavering toward Dylan's mother.

Pamela screamed, sprinting forward. Dylan watched her draw back her foot and kick Hunter's wrist hard. He heard the snap of the bone as the gun clattered to the floor. Symington cried out in pain but kept trying to throw off capture.

It felt as if the tableau had taken minutes to unfold, but he knew scant seconds had passed. Security personnel swarmed into the lobby, easily managing to subdue the cursing, enraged man struggling with Dylan.

"He didn't hurt you?"

It was his mother's voice asking that question but not of him. She had both hands on Pamela's shoulders, as if she needed to ensure herself that she was all right.

"Call Lieutenant Umberto," Dylan said as one of the security team helped him to his feet. "He was on his way to speak to this bastard at the office."

The chief of security nodded his head. "I'll see that Mr. Symington is handed over to him, sir."

"By the way, I'm fine, Mother," Dylan said, eyeing the way his mother was fussing over Pamela.

"Of course you are," his mother replied.

"He told me he had Eric murdered. That he used that Jeremy character to do it." Pamela stepped closer to him and threw her arms around his neck. Then she turned her head and smiled at Twyla. "Hey, little sister. Thanks for the tug."

"You didn't need my help. Not with these two watching out for you."

"Does this mean you don't think I'm a son of a bitch any longer?" Dylan asked her.

Twyla seemed to consider the matter and tossed his mother a cheeky grin for good measure. "I may have to reconsider."

"I'll call your father," his mother said. "We'll go upstairs, all of us, have some wine, and talk."

* * * *

The police had left them, after a good hour spent getting both Pamela's and Dylan's statements. Justin had arrived right after the police and hadn't left his wife's side. Now they were all trying to relax with that wine Maria promised having been delivered—along with a tray of hors d'oeuvres.

"I never knew he felt that way about me. I *never* looked at him, not in that way." Maria turned confused eyes to her husband. He reached out a hand and stroked her cheek, gently, then tucked her in close to his side. It was the same kind of gesture Dylan had used on her several times. His parents were so obviously in love with each other, she wondered how a man like Hunter Symington could ever have thought he could usurp Justin's place in Maria's life.

"I'm still in shock. I never would have suspected Hunter to be capable of the things he's done," Justin said in agreement.

Dylan's father was a handsome man. The silver wings at his temples and the laugh lines around his eyes added to his appeal. Pamela was certain, looking at the two men together, that Dylan would age equally well.

Pamela also noticed what the senior Pierce hadn't said—that he'd been shocked to learn of Dmitri's crimes. If Dylan had noticed, as well, he'd given no sign. Now, as Justin turned his attention to her, he asked, "Just who was Carmichael McRae to you, anyway?"

"Justin!" Maria pulled away from her husband and shot him an outraged look.

"Dad!" Dylan seemed equally aghast at the bold question

Pamela laughed, because both Maria and Dylan had protested in exactly the same tone of voice. Now that everything was over—now that Dylan had accepted her completely, without any explanations or reservations, she felt perfectly free to explain everything.

"He was my grandfather."

"And neither Neil nor Mary Ellen knew that?" Doubt lined his face. Justin had completely ignored his family's protests and seemed determined to know everything for himself.

"No, they didn't. We found each other—Carmichael and me—by accident. I'd gone to France after the death of my good friend and mentor, Arthur Kensington. I was touring one of the many galleries in Paris, and there he was. We seemed to hit it off and began to get together once a week to take in a different gallery. Then one day, I bent over to pick up something I'd dropped, and he saw my birthmark. I have a crescent-moon-shaped mark on the small of my back." She took a moment to look at Dylan, who winked at her in turn. She turned back to his father. "Apparently, it's a mark that runs in the McRae family. He invited me to his home for dinner. There, he told me about his son, who had rebelled against a planned future by running off—or as his generation called it, 'dropping out.' This was long before Carmichael moved to Paris. He had a picture of his son with an obviously pregnant woman. That woman was my mother.

"He didn't introduce me as his granddaughter to either his niece or his nephew, as he really didn't care for them at all. I met them once, when Carmichael took me to an art auction, and I found I agreed with his assessment of them. I didn't care about them, anyway. I only cared about learning about my father and getting to know my grandfather."

"And Kensington?" Dylan's expression was indulgent, and Pamela realized that he wasn't in the least surprised by her revelation. When she tilted her head to the side, he said, "When Mary Ellen made her dramatic exit in London, I noticed something on the small of her back, just above the cut of her gown. It wasn't, however, until I was on my way over here from Dmitri's that I realized what it was."

"Arthur Kensington was a friend of our foster father's," Twyla said. "And when Dad found out P.J. loved art, he had the man over to dinner so he could meet her."

"He became like an uncle to me, hiring me on to work in his gallery part-time when I turned sixteen. When I told him I wanted to be an art conservator—something he had trained for himself—he insisted on helping me. He and Elizabeth, his wife, never had kids. I guess I became the daughter he never had. When he died, he left me the gallery. His generosity floored me. I really wasn't expecting it at all."

"And Mulchaey hired you to work for him, didn't he?"

Pamela smiled at Dylan. "Yes. He had a couple of paintings that had been in his family's archives for generations, painted by one of his ancestors, which needed restoration. His offer came at a time when I wanted to be away from everyone and everything. The prospect of holing up on his estate was too good an offer to refuse."

"We haven't spoken of Dmitri." Maria reached out and put a hand on Dylan's arm. "I'm sorry."

"You have nothing to apologize for, Mother. You and Dad have been trying to tell me for a long time that he had problems. I refused to see them, and for that, *I'm* sorry."

"Your loyalty is one of your finest qualities," Pamela told him then. Placing a hand on his face, she didn't care if they had an audience or not. "I love you for a lot of reasons, but your loyalty and honor are at the top of the list."

"I think things are about to get sloppy here," Twyla said dryly.

"I am Greek. We are a passionate people. Sloppy is in my nature. So I am pleased that my future daughter-in-law is unafraid to show her feelings."

"You're just jealous," Pamela said to her sister. Then she turned her attention back to the man she loved. "But she's right. I'm feeling very sloppy. I love you, Dylan. And I don't even care if you do want to buy an entire island. I'll marry you, anyway."

"You just said so in front of witnesses. You're trapped now."

"I don't feel trapped. In fact, I feel as if, for the first time—well..." She laughed, shaking her head. "This is going to sound completely weird, but I feel as if, for the first time in *several* lifetimes, I'm finally, totally free."

"That's a nice coincidence," Dylan said softly as he pulled her close, "several lifetimes is precisely what I had in mind for us."

THE SEDUCTRESS
Song of the Sirens 1

THE END

WWW.MORGANASHBURY.COM

ABOUT THE AUTHOR

Morgan has been a writer since she was first able to pick up a pen. In the beginning it was a hobby, a way to create a world of her own, and who could resist the allure of that? Then as she grew and matured, life got in the way, as life often does. She got married and had three children, and worked in the field of accounting, for that was the practical thing to do and the children did need to be fed. And all the time she was being practical, she would squirrel herself away on quiet Sunday afternoons, and write.

Most children are raised knowing the Ten Commandments and the Golden Rule. Morgan's children also learned the Paper Rule: *thou shalt not throw out any paper that has thy mother's words upon it.* Believing in tradition, Morgan ensured that her children's children learned this rule, too.

Life threw Morgan a curve when, in 2002, she underwent emergency triple by-pass surgery. Second chances are to be cherished, and with the encouragement and support of her husband, Morgan decided to use hers to do what she'd always dreamed of doing: writing full time. "I can't tell you how much I love what I do. I am truly blessed."

Morgan has always loved writing romance. It is the one genre that can incorporate every other genre within its pulsating heart. Romance showcases all that human kind can aspire to be. And, she admits, she's a sucker for a happy ending.

Morgan's favorite hobbies are reading, cooking, and traveling— though she would rather you didn't mention that last one to her husband. She has too much fun teasing him about having become a "Traveling Fool" of late.

Morgan lives in Southwestern Ontario with a cat that has an attitude, a dog that has no dignity, and her husband of thirty-six years, David.

Siren Publishing, Inc.
www.SirenPublishing.com

Lightning Source UK Ltd.
Milton Keynes UK
16 July 2010

157136UK00006B/45/P